PATTERNS OF DECEIT

BY THOMAS SANFORD

authorHOUSE®

AuthorHouse™
1663 Liberty Drive
Bloomington, IN 47403
www.authorhouse.com
Phone: 1-800-839-8640

First published by AuthorHouse 6/9/2010

ISBN: 978-1-4520-2598-8 (e)
ISBN: 978-1-4520-2597-1 (sc)

Printed in the United States of America
Bloomington, Indiana

This book is printed on acid-free paper.

Dedication

To those who made
this novel possible -
especially William,
Eleanor, Judy, Bob,
my dedicated editor,
Marsha.
And to those who
made it necessary.

Characters
(In Alphabetical Order)

Jeremy Aycres	Associate Director of Research
Emory Beyer	Associate Director of Human Resources
Carl	Finance Department staff member
Kate Charles	Volunteer
Henry Davis	Associate Director of Security
Nicki English	Catering Manager, Dining Unlimited at Summerston
Trevor Erskine	Summerston Craft Festival sponsor
Brad Evans	Friend of Kate Charles
Serena Fields	Volunteer
Letitia Green	Assistant Manager, Membership Services
James Grover	Assistant to Thurston Wilde
Cora Halstead	Secretary, Membership Services
Jean Howard	Manager of Volunteers
Alfred Jackson	Museum Librarian
Edwina Jennings	Corporate Giving, Philanthropy Department
Judith Jordan	Summerston donor
Stewart Jordan	Judith's son
Daniel Kent	Director of Summerston
Donald Lewis	Chief Financial Officer
Jeffrey Longhurst	Chairman, Summerston Craft Festival Executive Committee
Elizabeth Markham	Dr. Kent's secretary

Andrew McAlister	Nephew of Arthur McAlister
Arthur McAlister	Original Summerston owner
Adrienne Monkton	Events Division Planner
Adam Payne	Chairman of Summerston Board of Trustees
Susan Penn	Volunteer
Rosalind Pepper	Manager, Public Relations
Elinor Pierson	Events Division Secretary
Theresa Redding	Friend of Adrienne Monkton
Julia Stevens	Manager, Membership Services
Harrison Tell	Former Director of Summerston
Nancy Brewster Veasel	Wife of Roland Veasel
Roland Veasel	Associate Director of Philanthropy
Thurston Wilde	Associate Director of Tours and Education

Summerston Museum of Folk Art Facilities

Williams House	Museum administrative offices
Richmond House	Summerston Craft Festival office

ONE

ood grief, fumed Adrienne Monkton as she hung up the phone. *He just never gives up.* Walking around her cluttered desk and skirting the piles of paper and boxes that adorned her office floor, she headed out the door and down the stairway. "Guess what Roland wants changed now?" she called to her secretary, Elinor Pierson, as she passed into the kitchen.

Elinor left her desk in the next room and joined her. "What's going on?"

"You remember during the meeting last month the executive committee okayed our using Green Jasmine for the preview party, and Roland agreed? Everyone was crazy about the menu, and the price was extremely reasonable. The table linen color scheme was perfect and very different from anything we have done. The owner was excited about being selected - it would mean great PR for the restaurant. I was to sign and return the contract today."

"You're not telling me Roland has decided we can't use Green Jasmine?" asked Elinor.

"More like he has ordered me not to. Absolutely forbids it. Says we have to get a bid from and use Dining Unlimited," she said naming the museum's food service provider. "He contends it looks bad to use anyone else." Adrienne was thoroughly disgusted.

"Certainly he knows they always charge twice as much as anyone else, and the food is not as creative. Remember how Nicki tried to over-charge Howland Enterprises when their president wanted to hold that huge Christmas party here last year? She eventually cut the price in half once she realized Dining Unlimited and the museum would lose their business. It was really disgraceful."

"Of course, Roland knows. He is tight with Nicki - they go way back to his work at the hospital - and you know he was part of the team negotiating Dining Unlimited's new contract with the museum. Talk about a conflict of interest!"

"How do you think the committee members will react? They want the budget cut at least twenty percent, but if you have to use Dining Unlimited, that will be hard to do. Food is a major expense. There are only a few other areas where you can trim the budget."

Adrienne took her lunch out of the refrigerator and grabbed a bottle of raspberry flavored water. "I'll get a quote from Nicki. If the usual inflated costs show up, Roland will find out very quickly that the committee won't accept them."

TWO

As Adrienne went back up the winding staircase carrying her lunch, a sleek black crow flew out of the poplar tree next to the stone wall bordering the driveway. He soared over the now brown fields, crossed the woodland naked of leaves and settled on the slate roof of a three story stone building a quarter mile away. Across the cobblestone circle from where he sat rose the world famous Summerston Museum of Folk Art - a combination of nineteenth and twentieth century buildings artfully blended into each other and housing the collections of Arthur and Andrew McAlister.

In 1914, Arthur McAlister purchased a nine hundred acre farm and during the next six years he added the four surrounding properties, creating an estate well over two thousand acres which he named "Summerston". Fields and woods dotted the rolling hillsides, a small stream flowed through the property and five deep ponds, attracting birds and wildlife, added to its beauty. He renovated and enlarged the original farm house, creating a fifty-room mansion filled with his collection of folk art. Arthur was not only passionate about collecting but about gardening. He invited prominent American horticulturalists to advise him and together they created an almost seventy-acre retreat with gardens representing all of the seasons. The grounds surrounding his home were always filled with color, even in the winter when bright red holly berries set off the blues and greens of the conifers.

In addition to the farm house in which Arthur lived, his land purchases provided him with a number of houses, barns and out buildings. The houses he leased to employees. The barns and farming fields he leased to area farmers.

Arthur lived alone. His wife died several years after their marriage, and they had no children. However, he was very close to his only sibling, a brother, whose family he frequently entertained. His nephew, Andrew, especially enjoyed spending time with Arthur, and under his guidance quickly developed an enthusiastic interest in folk art. They both appreciated the decorative and practical aspects of the genre and found the actual collecting to be exhilarating. Each looked forward to the thrill of the chase - searching for specific pieces and attending auctions. By his mid-thirties Andrew had amassed his own sizeable collection.

Following Arthur's death in 1950, Andrew inherited the estate. Not wishing to manage such a large property, he donated all but the original nine hundred acres for public and private uses that guaranteed their preservation. The will provided an endowment for the creation of a museum to make Arthur's collection available for public display, and Andrew spent the next five years making that a reality.

In 1955 The Summerston Museum of Folk Art opened to the public. It featured the fifty-room mansion filled with Arthur's extraordinary collection in period settings and traditional displays and the extensive garden that surrounded it. In addition, the estate included a new wing housing Andrew's collection, a library, restoration work rooms and offices. A number of the original out buildings were renovated as a visitor reception center, cafeteria, administrative offices and a gift shop. Arthur had a grey stone house and small guest cottage built on the north west corner of the property for himself.

Under Andrew's guidance Summerston became a remarkable resource. Collectors found a world-renowned two-century collection, researchers a comprehensive library, and those in need of conservation assistance a state-of-the art laboratory - all staffed with dedicated curators and conservationists. Those seeking nature's beauty found an English-style country garden to refresh the soul. But even the Garden of Eden had its serpent, and Summerston would soon be no different.

The first director was a retired university dean who was not only a successful fundraiser but a skillful manager, able to coordinate the efforts of staff members with varied interests and expertise. Andrew and he were childhood friends, and Andrew trusted him explicitly. Nonetheless, Andrew still enjoyed walking in the garden, joining a guided tour, dining in the cafeteria or observing the work on a delicate restoration project. He demanded perfection, but he respected his staff and looked out for their interests. His hand picked board of trustees understood that he expected them to pay careful attention to all of the details involved with running such a museum.

After he died in 1980, things began to change. Personal friends of Andrew's who shared his vision, both for the museum and its staff, retired from the board. They were replaced by collectors whose dedication to the workings of the museum did not match their enthusiasm for folk art. A series of directors with excellent resumes but more self-promoting managerial styles were hired by a board that took a hands off approach.

The current director, Dr. Daniel Kent, was recruited when the problems with his predecessor became so flagrant that the board finally had to take notice. Known to the trustees, and because of the urgency of the situation, he was immediately hired with no competitive process. Encouraged by Dr. Kent's promise to promote staff initiative and creativity at Summerston, the board naively returned to its former *laissez faire* approach.

THREE

In an office just below the crow's perch sat Roland Veasel, Adrienne's boss and confidant of Dr. Kent. An always impeccably well-dressed man with a trademark bow tie, he was in his mid-fifty's. His prematurely grey hair and affected wire-rimmed glasses gave him a scholarly appearance, and his well-rehearsed smile created the illusion of friendliness. He was neither. Nor was he the sophisticate his style of dress would indicate. A long-time friend of the director, to whom he owed his position, Roland was a schemer who spent more time covering his tracks and taking credit for the work of his staff than doing any himself. In only two short years as Associate Director of Philanthropy he had created a paralyzing hostile environment within his department - similar to that which marked his twenty-five year tenure at Leland University's hospital. Those with class, talent and initiative had either left the museum or been "laid off". Those remaining did so out of fear that they would be unable to secure another job given the current economic downturn.

Roland oversaw all fund raising activities at Summerston including two annual fundraisers - the Summerston Craft Festival and The Textile Market. Adrienne Monkton was responsible for the organization of these events.

On this cold day at the end of January, she was occupied with the details of the craft festival which was held each May.

As the crow flew off toward the garden to dine at one of the bird feeders maintained by the horticultural staff, Roland's phone rang.

"Roland, are we still on for lunch?" asked Thurston Wilde, Associate Director of Tours and Education.

"I was just getting ready to leave. Meet me out front in about 10 minutes, and we can walk over to the visitor center together," Roland suggested. "Can't wait to tell you about my latest shot fired over dear Adrienne's bow," he laughed.

"Delicious," Thurston laughed in return.

FOUR

R oland left his office and climbed a short flight of stairs to put letters in the department mail basket. As he passed the first office on the left - now empty - he frowned. That had not gone at all well. The former tenant hadn't stayed even a year. Hired to court and encourage wealthy donors to remember Summerston generously in their wills, Ross Richmond hadn't been ideal for the task. A quiet, well spoken man in his early forties he was not the usual extrovert found in fundraising positions, but he was easily intimidated, easily managed. A week ago, Ross had announced that he had taken a position with one of the area's community colleges and was giving his two-week notice. Already short staffed due to the departure of another employee, on the pretense that she was pursuing a masters degree, Roland had been furious.

"Just leave now," he had yelled at Ross, unable to conceal his anger. "There is no point in your hanging around here for the next two weeks."

For his part, Ross had been more than happy to leave immediately. He was becoming increasingly nervous and had developed periodic migraine headaches working for Roland. When a friend recommended him for a development position at the college and he was hired, he had been delighted to join several other former Summerston employees who had found refuge there.

At least, in Roland's view, there was one silver lining with the departure of Ross and Alice. Most departments had been forced to lay off employees in September with more trimming predicted before the end of the fiscal year. Because the Philanthropy Department had already lost several employees, Dr. Kent had all but told Roland his department was exempt from the second round. However, Roland did not share this information with his staff and even taunted them at the monthly departmental meeting in October.

"You best stay very busy and look like you are irreplaceable," he had warned.

He went on to relate how he had been forced to lay off a long-time staff member - a very troublesome woman in his unspoken opinion - and that the experience had been most difficult.

"While I know it is hard on the employees being let go, it is even harder on the supervisors who have to deliver the bad news. They are also most deserving of your empathy."

Everyone was quite appalled by Roland's comments - this was a new low, even for him. And especially so when they later learned that the employee Roland "laid off" was actually retired with her full pension.

FIVE

As Thurston left his office in the museum building and headed for Williams House to meet Roland, Jeremy Aycres, Associate Director of Research, was entering the cafeteria. A little over six-feet tall and slim, he had a full head of brown hair and kind green eyes. Dressed like a college professor, he always appeared slightly rumpled - his tie was often askew or his shirt not completely tucked in. Had a vote been taken among the staff, he would have won hands down as the most considerate, respected and thoughtful supervisor. While the administrative managers' styles of fear and intimidation promoted antipathy, his management style was one of mutual respect that encouraged loyalty to the museum. Self-promotion might reign in other departments, but in Research it was all about promoting Summerston.

At lunch, Jeremy tended to avoid the administrative managers, always selecting a table in the cafeteria as far away from them as possible. Staffers often teased him about sitting in solitary splendor in the corner next to a potted palm. But while kidding him in a good natured way about his holding court, it was not a joke when they looked across the room, saw Dr. Kent and referred to him as "The Monarch". Jeremy's assistant had suggested that the drawings Jeremy produced should show Dr. Kent as a large yellow and black butterfly with a tiny crown on its head.

Jeremy relied on his interest in bird watching and his skills as an illustrator to survive the monthly senior staff meetings, filled with sarcasm and double entendres from the administrative section. Resting on his lap, out of sight, his notebook contained more than announcements or policy changes presented by Dr. Kent. Some days it featured the director, himself, as a peregrine falcon wearing glasses and carrying a laptop computer. He was usually flanked by two large turkey buzzards or two bats, wings folded, hanging upside down, but always sporting Roland and Thurston's colorful bow ties. The red-haired associate director of the garden became a red-headed woodpecker complete with green wellies and carrying a rake. He was less kind to the head of public relations, Rosalind Pepper, who morphed into a catbird wearing a miniature witch's hat, with a small broom tucked under its wing. The only Summerston staffer who had seen the drawings was his assistant. When he asked Jeremy how he perceived himself, Jeremy drew a small wren, sparrow or house finch - all prey for raptor birds.

Once, Jeremy had gotten so carried away with these portrayals that upon entering Roland's office to talk with him, his eyes had gone not to the desk chair but up to the brass chandelier, expecting to see Roland hanging upside down from one of its arms.

SIX

Looking not unlike Jeremy's portrayal, in a black coat and matching cashmere scarf, Roland met Thurston outside Williams House. They walked quickly through the garden to the visitor center which faced a large meadow. In the spring its colorful landscape of wild flowers enchanted visitors. The building, once a dairy barn, now housed the reception area and gift shop. An addition, with open floor plan and matching soaring ceiling, featured a cafeteria and several smaller dining rooms. Passing the tall cafeteria windows, Roland and Thurston were forced to step aside as a middle-aged couple came out the door.

"Imagine not offering a garden-only ticket when they advertise the garden and encourage visitors to walk its paths and enjoy its beauty year-round," grumbled the husband.

"First museum with a garden we have ever toured that makes you buy the whole package," his wife added. "And we have traveled the world."

Thurston rolled his eyes at Roland. He was responsible for visitor services but had little interest in what visitors actually wanted. He provided the usual staff-training seminars - hiring outside consultants who used yellow smiley faces, role playing exercises and Power Point presentations. While such sessions offered general advice for working with the public, they lacked an understanding of the issues actually pertaining to Summerston, itself. And Thurston cared little for suggestions from his staff who did understand the issues. Long lines of visitors due to unnecessarily complicated ticketing procedures and insufficient staffing were not his concern. Truth be known, this was not his area of expertise. He delegated staff supervision to his assistant, James Grover, who shared Thurston's lack of interest in advice from those on the front line.

While Thurston headed for the gift shop to pick up a book order he had placed, Roland stopped at the ticket desk.

"Aside from those attending the quilt seminar, have we had many visitors today?" he asked the attractive lady seated at the end of the counter.

"Quiet, as usual for January," replied Serena Fields, a long-time volunteer who sold museum memberships.

Taking a closer look at her Roland said, "What a beautiful shawl you are wearing today, Serena. It compliments your hair."

"Thank you," she replied, with little enthusiasm. She was not taken in by his flattery. Like staff members, even the part-time volunteers had learned what was behind that friendly facade. When Roland arrived at Summerston, he feigned a keen interest in the concerns and ideas of the volunteers working in his department. They were all impressed that someone in upper management appeared to respect their talents and opinions - many had impressive credentials in business, government and non-profits. When their responsibilities dramatically diminished, they realized that he had only used their information to criticize his staff. Now in fear that a volunteer might make an error for which they would be blamed, managers kept tight control over all volunteer activities. Those working with the public had few responsibilities and were permitted to use no initiative. Finding this demeaning, Serena had recently decided to limit her volunteer time at Summerston to special events. This was her last assignment for Membership Services. A number of other volunteers had left the museum entirely.

As Roland moved away, Serena turned to Patricia, responsible for ticketing, and grimaced.

"I have never met a man who took such an interest in my clothing. He is always saying something about my shoes matching my dress or checking the style of blouse I have on. My late husband was always very complimentary, but this is just plain peculiar - like talking with a budding fashion designer."

"It would seem more natural coming from Thurston," her companion laughed. "He thinks he sets the style around here."

"I guess this is one of Thurston's weeks to be in town," Serena commented. Thurston's frequent absences from the museum were often discussed.

"He has some kind of a special arrangement with the museum, but personally I don't understand why."

Serena just shook her head. "He was supposed to know all the right people and bring in large contributions. Remember how his photograph was all over the museum's magazine when he first arrived? He always had his arm around Monsieur this and Madame de whatever."

"Very little, if anything, ever came of those contacts.

He lead a couple of tours to Europe and England for the museum's upper level donors, and they did meet members of the British peerage. However, it soon became apparent that the French counts and English lords needed to maintain their own chateaux or manors and were not keen on sending money here."

"And his photo just as quickly disappeared from the museum's magazine," Serena wryly noted.

"While Thurston's star may not be as bright here, apparently others are enamored with him. My daughter, who lives in San Francisco, sent me an article about him from The Grayson Museum's monthly magazine. He gave one of his lectures there and, according to the author, charmed the audience."

Serena took the article out of her tote bag and passed it along the counter to Patricia.

SEVEN

L ooking at the article, Patricia was struck by the
glossy photograph of a broadly smiling Thurston.
Wearing a silk and wool blend beige jacket, chocolate brown slacks, white shirt and startling yellow print
bow tie, he leaned casually against one of two stone lions
flanking a wide outside staircase. His resemblance to a
landed English nobleman was, undoubtedly, the aristocratic appearance he sought. According to the adjacent
text, Thurston Wilde grew up in Chicago and majored
in art history at Princeton. He wrote his masters thesis
on Reuben Moulthrop, an 18th and 19th century folk
artist known for having waxworks of full-size figures that
toured the country. Following graduation he worked as a
curator at museums in San Francisco, Chicago and New
York. Realizing that the average person was more interested in the personal life of an artist than in his technique,
he began researching the lives of American folk artists.
Coupling this with a theatrical heritage, he developed a
series of lectures which he delivered at colleges, universi-
ties and museum seminars.

Short on details, the article neglected the more colorful aspects of Thurston's life - the type of details about
artists that he, himself, expounded upon with great rel-

ish when lecturing. He was the only child of a musical comedy star and her husband, a talented dancer. While appearing on Broadway in minor roles, they often starred in road company productions. The unplanned arrival of a child only sidelined his mother for less than a year. Six months after his birth, she left Thurston with her wealthy mother-in-law in Chicago, to join her husband on stage in a revival of *Guys and Dolls* opening in Seattle. Understanding that trying to raise a child on the road was unrealistic and being sympathetic to their passion for the theater, Mrs. Wilde readily agreed to raise Thurston. She had confided to her best friend that having a child around was, in fact, most welcome. Her late husband had passed away three years before, and she was lonely.

The senior Mrs. Wilde's penthouse apartment on Lake Shore Drive covered two floors and was more than sufficient to accommodate a suite for Thurston and a full time nanny as well as rooms for the live-in couple who looked after her needs. She doted on Thurston and gave him the best of everything. While other children visited the zoo, she took him to Africa on a photography safari. Since he enjoyed the aquarium, she took him to the Caribbean where he learned to scuba dive, and later to the Great Barrier Reef. His favorite museum of all was The Field Museum of Natural History, and she signed up for the family adventure trips it sponsored.

To encourage an interest in art, she enrolled him in classes at The Art Institute and took him to all of the local museums. From an early age, it became apparent that he shared her interest which delighted her. They toured the most famous museums of North America, Europe and Asia together. At college while his declared major was art history, it was not surprising that he minored in theater arts. His freshman roommate, Romy, was the son of an Italian count from Venice. They became instant and lifelong friends. After his sophomore year, Romy returned to Italy, and Thurston studied abroad in London the first semester and in Paris the second. They met frequently, and Romy introduced Thurston to his family and friends, many of whom were members of the aristocracy in Italy, France and England. It was these contacts which made Thurston a very attractive asset to any museum and one of the reasons the former Summerston director, Harrison Tell, hired him.

Attending a three day seminar in Chicago, Harrison heard one of Thurston's very entertaining lectures and sat with him at several dinners. He was impressed not only with his somewhat flamboyant style but by his name dropping. Usually, Harrison found this annoying, but if Thurston truly knew all of these wealthy patrons of the arts, he was someone to be cultivated. At Summerston Thurston could acquaint his aristocratic friends with the museum and woo wealthy local donors with his wit and introductions to the nobility of Europe and Great Britain. And almost as important, he was someone that the director could control. From their conversations, Harrison got the distinct impression that Thurston was interested in elevated job titles but not in the supervisory responsibilities they entailed.

Returning to the museum, Harrison did a little research and discovered that Thurston had the contacts about which he had bragged. After a series of telephone conversations, Thurston agreed to come to Summerston. The salary offered was not what he requested, but they worked out an arrangement which permitted him to supplement his museum salary with an almost unlimited number of off-site lectures. On the surface it was an ideal arrangement for both Thurston and the museum.

EIGHT

While the two ladies finished reading the article, its subject rejoined Roland, and they went into the cafeteria. Leaving their coats and scarves on two chairs surrounding one of the small round tables, Thurston and Roland walked into the serving area. Thurston read the menu for hot entrees, but Roland decided to make himself a salad. Today the offerings were more to his liking. Some days they appeared quite inedible. Nicki English, Catering Manager for Dining Unlimited, had assured him that even though he did not find the hummus and grilled eggplant visually pleasing, they were quite healthy. He remained unconvinced.

He stood in a short line, tray in hand, and looked around the cafeteria. No more than thirty people sat in small groups at tables scattered throughout the large open area. Most were staff members, identified by their security badges. Less than a dozen appeared to be visitors, and the majority of them looked uninspiring. *Why do tourists have to be so sloppy?* he thought. *It used to be people got dressed up to go out in public or, at least, put on something that was presentable.* A large, overweight man carrying a tray laden with dishes made his way to a table by the window. His tight red tee shirt boasted: "I skinny dipped at Lake Como". *Now there's an image that doesn't bear thinking about*, he grimaced.

As Roland filled his plate with field greens, tomatoes, cucumbers and sliced chicken, he continued inwardly to grumble about the type of tourists coming to the museum. If he had his way, only those with intelligence and a genuine interest in folk art would be admitted. Collectors and researchers, not the riffraff he saw in the cafeteria today.

How Roland had become so intolerant and incurably snobbish often puzzled his late parents. Growing up in a small Midwestern town he had been taught acceptance and appreciation of everyone. He went to school with children from lower to upper class families. No matter who they were, his classmates were always welcome in their home.

Roland had earned a partial scholarship to a prominent New England university and declared a business major at the end of his sophomore year. When he returned home for the summer after that second year, his father had noted a change. Living in a big city, exposed to different races, economic levels and foreign students should have broadened his outlook. Unfortunately, it did just the opposite. He joined a fraternity that had a reputation for social status exclusivity and was not the stereotypical party hearty house. In April of his junior year, he announced he would not be returning home for the summer and, instead, found a job at a private country club.

During Roland's graduation weekend at Leland University, his proud parents, brother and sister found him somewhat aloof. Impeccably dressed, he seemed a little embarrassed by their respectable but not fashionable attire. Although they were dutifully introduced to his fraternity brothers and their parents, all of whom appeared affluent, no dinners or luncheons were planned. His parents had been looking forward to becoming better acquainted with his friends, and his younger sister was hoping to impress one of his handsome classmates. While not impolite or unkind to them, Roland had no intention of including his family in what he considered his new, more sophisticated life.

Using his fraternity connections Roland was able to secure a job with a major non-profit organization. More interested in learning who had money and who could help him advance his career, he spent little time learning the basics of fundraising. Instead, he made sure he was involved with the charity's galas and smaller fundraisers where he was most likely to meet the right people. It became well known in the office that he passed the less glamorous jobs onto others, especially interns or volunteers, citing seniority or more pressing duties. Dealing with mailings, phone solicitations or budget preparations were too mundane and of little interest to someone with Roland's lofty aspirations.

After several years at the charity, a friend told him about an opening in development at the renowned hospital associated with his alma mater. Using recommendations from influential contacts made at the charity, he applied and was hired. The department was quite large, and he was one of several employees responsible for soliciting alumnae to finance the latest addition. He made sure to include on his solicitation list the names of former fraternity brothers to insure a successful result. A number had fared extremely well in a very short time and were responsive to his appeal to their loyalty and to their vanity when he suggested having a waiting room, patient library or chapel named for them.

Roland often dined with his fraternity brothers, not out of friendship but to acquire more names of donors whose generosity he could tap. Out of his hearing, other employees complained of his pirating names from their lists and contacting the potential donors before those assigned to do so could call. Obviously, not everyone on Roland's list was receptive to his approach. Unwilling to waste his time on them, Roland avoided calling anyone he did not know, simply checking them off as non-donors.

His supervisor found it curious that Roland always completed his calling much faster than anyone else. But Roland's results were exemplary; so he did not question it. The less than complimentary comments made by other staff members were attributed to jealousy. When Roland volunteered to represent the department at special hospital functions for major donors, it was assumed he was a dedicated employee. Roland, however, had a different reason for attending, viewing such events as self-promoting opportunities for himself.

It was at one of these functions that he met his future wife.

NINE

Escorting her widowed father to a donor appreciation party, Nancy Brewster was bored listening to his friends discuss their golf scores or latest investment coups. Holding a glass of white wine, she let her mind wander. The recent successful defense of her doctoral thesis meant that she could now concentrate on her research. At the corporate laboratory where she worked, Nancy and her colleagues were focusing on the development of artificial finger joints. Having watched her mother suffer from arthritis and become unable to pursue her beloved hobby of knitting, this was a cause close to Nancy's heart.

Refocusing on the conversation around her, she heard her father suggest they have something to eat from the buffet before they move on to the concert in the university's impressive music building. Ahead of her in line was a young man she remembered seeing at one of the earlier functions she had attended. Handsome and dressed more stylishly than most men his age, he piqued her interest. As he turned to put dressing on his salad, she noticed his name tag identified him as a member of the hospital development staff. He looked up at her and smiled.

"I hope you and your father are enjoying the evening

so far, Ms Brewster," Roland inquired, quickly reading her name tag. He had developed the skill of appearing not to read a tag, making the person to whom he was speaking think he remembered them.

"Yes we are, thank you," she responded.

He made a point of moving only a short distance away and watching where she and her father went after they left the buffet table. At the same time he was searching his memory for what he knew about them. Was it worth spending time with them?

He recalled that her father was a member of a prestigious law firm in town and her mother came from a very wealthy New England family. The Brewsters traced their roots back to the Mayflower and had occupied the same lake-front house since the mid-nineteenth century. Except, of course, for the six month period after a family of squirrels had taken possession while Nancy's parents were on a five week cruise. Their dining on the electrical wires and using insulation for nesting materials had rendered the house inhabitable and in need of complete renovation. Definitely donors to add to his list of conquests - Nancy and her father, not the squirrels.

After speaking to several other diners, he approached the table where they sat with another couple. "May I join you?" he asked Mr. Brewster. Invited to sit down, he engaged everyone in conversation until it was time to walk the short distance to the music building.

He had found Nancy to be out-spoken and not a little sarcastic. A challenge, he thought. But not an unpleasant one. With her connections she could be extremely useful. At the end of the evening, he sought her out and asked if she would like to have dinner with him the next week. She agreed.

As the months went by Nancy was flattered by his interest in her career and impressed by the restaurants or art exhibitions he selected. For his part, he made it a point to learn about the things which were important to her. She was better educated and smarter, from a very different, very privileged background and knew everyone. But in some ways, they were quite alike. He enjoyed her sharp wit and, at times, biting criticism of others - not unlike his own observations.

After a courtship of eighteen months, they were married in a relatively small ceremony. Nancy was not into big statements or fancy parties. This disappointed Roland. He had hoped for a chance to mingle with her family's important friends. Eventually, he was able to convince Nancy that her father should introduce them formally as was the usual custom. While the actual wedding reception was limited to a small number of family and friends, Mr. Brewster hosted a large cocktail party in the ballroom of one of the city's finest hotels following their honeymoon trip to Aruba.

Over the years, through Nancy's family connections, Roland continued his career as a successful fundraiser for the hospital. It did not bother him that when he called a potential donor, he was known as Nancy Brewster's husband. He moved up in the department and became manager of corporate and special gifts. When a new administrator, Dr. Daniel Kent, arrived at the hospital, Roland made sure he understood that Roland was the person in Development who knew everyone. One of Roland's main responsibilities was to prepare guest lists for hospital events. He told Dr. Kent that he could brief him prior to such events, insuring that the hospital president knew which donors required personal attention. Coming from the west and unfamiliar with the important families in the area, he gratefully accepted Roland's recommendation. It was not long before Dr. Kent was relying on Roland and, seemingly, in his debt for his own success as a fundraiser.

A debt he repaid when Dr. Kent retired from the university hospital twenty years later, and his successor was on the verge of replacing Roland. The new president, Evan Griswald, was from the area and did not need anyone's help identifying potential donors or those needing coddling. In addition, Mr. Griswald had taken an instant dislike to Roland during their first meeting. Using his influence with the Summerston board of trustees, Dr. Kent secured the then-vacant position of Associate Director of Philanthropy for Roland. Spun as if he had been courted and lured away from the hospital, Roland's arrival at the museum was heralded as a coup for Summerston by Director Harrison Tell. The development staff he had supervised at the hospital viewed it more as a coup d'etat and celebrated his departure.

TEN

Nancy had been relieved to learn that Dr. Kent had stepped in to insure Roland would have something to occupy his time. The idea that Mr. Griswold would replace him, leaving Roland without a job did not bear thinking about.

While Roland prospered in donor development, Nancy continued her work in medical research, taking time off to give birth to a son and a daughter. They were now living three thousand miles away, by personal choice as much as by their career choices. Since the children had moved out of the house, there had been little to keep the marriage intact. Except for Roland's reputation and the need to avoid scandal. By tacit understanding they remained together with Nancy attending public functions when necessary. She actually enjoyed meeting the more interesting donors both at the hospital and now at Summerston.

In spite of their efforts to maintain the facade of normalcy in public, among their friends, it was common knowledge that it was a marriage in name only. Nancy was glad that her father had died five years earlier so that he could not see the turn her life had taken. However, truth be told, she was not unhappy. She enjoyed her research, spending time with old friends and now spending time with a new friend. When she left on weekend trips, Roland did not ask where she was going.

His announcement four years ago that he had finally found his true self and knew that he was not interested in women did not surprise her. She had suspected it for some time. What did surprise her was his lack of discretion. He had become infatuated with a waiter at the local yacht club. The young man did not return his feelings and eventually consulted the club's manager. Roland was warned that a court-issued restraining order would be sought if he did not stop contacting the waiter. And Roland would, of course, be barred from the club.

After that, Roland realized he had foolishly put his position at the hospital in jeopardy. For someone as calculating and controlled as Roland, this was quite a self-revelation. And one he took to heart. From now on, there would be not even a hint of scandal. Any liaisons would be conducted with the utmost discretion.

ELEVEN

For Thurston such discretion was not a problem. He was comfortable with himself and his life style. It amused him to overhear talk about his frequent lunches with Roland both at and away from the museum. While not currently in a permanent relationship, he was not interested in Roland except as a colleague. One had only to note the preponderance of women in their departments to understand why the men tended to stick together.

One such female staff member was Julia Stevens, Manager of Membership Services, who reported to Roland. While he and Thurston finished lunch and then returned to their offices, she was reviewing her plan for an upcoming exhibition preview party. *From Soaring Eagles to Strutting Roosters - 19th century Weathervanes* was due to open April 10 and the party would be held the night before. During the past several years as departments were pared down, responsibilities were consolidated. Now Julia handled not only membership but all exhibition previews. Like so many other employees at Summerston who had seen their duties expand into areas not within their expertise, Julia was very uncomfortable as a party planner. Over the years these previews rarely strayed from their rather dull, unimaginative model. Name tags were dispensed, cocktails served, seasonal hors d'oeuvres passed, guests viewed the exhibitions, and staff mingled in the hope of encouraging additional donations. Occasionally, a lecture preceded the exhibition's viewing.

In spite of this routine sameness, Julia always found herself in a nervous state, unable to quell the fears that she or her staff would do something wrong and upset Roland or Dr. Kent. Her unease was shared by her assistant, Letitia Green. With an obsessive compulsive disposition, Letitia often drove her co-workers crazy. Although she had a reputation at the museum as a procrastinator, in reality, she spent so much time worrying about minutia that she could never meet a deadline.

Julia left her office and stopped by Letitia's. Intimidated by her almost sterile office with everything lined up precisely, Julia suggested they meet in the conference room.

"Cora," she called to her secretary, "please join us. We need to go over the preview plan before I submit it to Roland."

Cora Halstead, had been at Summerston for 15 years and was the complete opposite of her two colleagues - unruffled, practical and superbly organized. If you needed something involving membership handled efficiently, everyone at the museum knew to call her.

"Now, here is what I have in mind," Julia explained, distributing copies of her plan. "I have spoken with Nicki, and she is handling the cocktail hour. She will oversee everything; so we don't have to worry about that. Letitia, I need you to get me the list we'll use for the invitations - complimentary and paying guests. To keep down expenses, we will have to start at the $500 membership level for comps this time. With the budget cuts, there won't be any kind of a lecture or entertainment. Cora, you should order the name tags. Once we know who is coming, you can print them out."

"What has Publicity come up with for the invitation design?" asked Letitia. "The last one was pretty ordinary. I thought things would change when Dr. Kent came on board."

Julia pulled a copy of the invitation out of her folder and passed it around. For years invitations to events at Summerston had been almost collectors items, featuring appropriately themed designs. When Dr. Kent's predecessor, the youthful Harrison Tell, arrived as director, he had surprised everyone by insisting upon State Department-like formal invitations. Perhaps that should have been an early indication of Harrison's personal lack of creativity and his resentment of anyone on the staff who exhibited it.

"Are we using the mail house to send these out?" asked Cora. "Or do you want me to call in a group of volunteers to stuff the envelopes and attach address labels?"

"To be on the safe side, we'll use the mail house. Then if there is any kind of a problem, it won't be our fault," Julia responded.

"What about staffing the preview? Are we all to be there, and do we need help?" Letitia wondered. She did not enjoy the previews, finding most of the guests uninformed about art of any kind and boring to talk to. Why come to an exhibition at such a famous museum and not know anything or even want to be educated? To be seen, of course. Such a waste.

"Cora, contact the volunteers who usually help us out with these. We only need two to staff the name tag table. And don't call Rachel - she was so annoying the last time trying to show us how to organize the name tags. We've done this often enough, we certainly know what we are doing."

Cora would have liked to tell Julia that their system was quite inefficient, creating long lines of guests waiting for their name tags. And that Rachel would never help again because of how rudely she had been treated by a staff member at a previous event. The employee had since left, but Rachel could not be persuaded to return to Summerston. That was a shame because she had been an event organizer for a major insurance company and knew exactly how things could be done efficiently and with real class.

"Have I missed anything? Roland wants our plan this afternoon. I'm sure, no matter what we propose, he will find something wrong. He always does."

No one had anything to add, and the meeting ended. Julia went down the hall and left the plan in Roland's office. She was relieved to find him absent.

TWELVE

Several days later, shortly after four o'clock in the afternoon, Rosalind Pepper, Manager of Public Relations, climbed slowly up the stairs, her heavy coat flapping open. Not one to spend any time keeping physically fit, she resented the walk from her office to Williams House followed by a climb up the steep flight of stairs. *This is such a pain. He could have dropped by my office while he was gossiping with Thurston earlier today. So typical of the…*

"Hello, Roland, I brought you the publicity proofs for the craft festival brochure as requested," she explained as Roland Veasel suddenly appeared above her and descended the few stairs from the upper level to his office.

Without a word he preceded her into his office and sat behind the desk. Neglecting to ask her to take off her coat or sit down, he put his hand out for the folder she was holding.

"I'll take a look at this when I have time," he said placing the file on his desk.

"The printer needs the brochure in a week in order to send it off to the mail house on time."

"Understood. Now, I want to be clear about something. Every piece of publicity for the craft festival, no matter what it is, comes directly to me. It does not go to Adrienne. I will discuss it with her after I have had a chance to review it. Tell that to anyone in your department who is handling the event's PR," he said, looking at Rosalind for the first time.

No fan of Adrienne's, she was happy to comply.

"I understand and will pass the word," she said. Realizing that Roland had nothing more to say to her, she left his office, descended the stairs and went out into the fading winter daylight.

On her way back to her office, she couldn't help but wonder what Roland was up to. No stranger to deception, Rosalind was not greatly admired at the museum. Most curators who worked with her on exhibition publicity found her disagreeable, uncooperative and, at times, disingenuous.

She was aware that Roland did not pay close attention to the minute details one needed to know when reviewing publicity materials. It was impossible for him to determine whether the text was accurate or if the photographs were appropriate. He must be trying to cause trouble for Adrienne. And that suited Rosalind just fine.

Adrienne greatly annoyed her because Adrienne did pay close attention to details, did know when something was not correct and did not hesitate to point it out. She also had a sense of design and was often critical of what Rosalind's department produced - not creative enough, no pizzaz, not eye catching, too complex.

Rosalind was not one to admit, even to herself, her short comings or those of her brow-beaten staff. But it was no secret, the materials produced by her department, when compared to publicity pieces from other area museums, lacked originality and were too often cluttered and confusing.

Rosalind was one more example of the mediocrity rising to the top at Summerston. Her former boss, an arrogant, unpleasant man had been laid off the previous fall. Everyone who dealt with him had breathed a sigh of relief when he left - until she had been promoted. Several talented long-time employees, any of whom should have been elevated, were now forced to work for a far less qualified supervisor with less seniority. But one easily manipulated, one who would not question authority from those to whom she was beholden for her promotion.

THIRTEEN

After Rosalind's departure, Roland wandered up the stairs and into the office of Edwina Jennings, responsible for corporate donations in the Philanthropy Department. She was extremely busy and not pleased to see him. However, he sat down, made himself comfortable and asked her how things were going.

"Just fine," she replied. "I have confirmed the sponsors for The Textile Market in the fall. We will have the same ones as last year. In spite of the economy, they are willing to repeat."

"They like being associated with Summerston; so it isn't surprising."

For the next half an hour he talked about all manner of things, just gossiping and generally wasting time. During the past year, he had gotten into the habit of chatting with her and trying out ideas. Eventually, Edwina had realized that he was using her to get information about people in the museum. She was not adverse to a bit of gossip, but his visits had gotten to be a problem because their frequency was interfering with her work. Obviously, he did not have enough to do. But he was her boss; so she could hardly object.

He also often used her as a secretary. He no longer

had one, having worked very hard to force Cynthia to quit. When he came to the museum, she had been assigned to him. Finding she could not please him no matter what she did, she tried to talk with him about what he wanted. Rather than spelling out how he liked things done, he told her to go to Human Resources and ask them. She found this very odd, but she met with Emory Beyer, the head of HR, and explained the situation. Much to her surprise, instead of helping her, he asked her if she wanted to quit. She was stunned. She did not like working for Roland, but she needed the job. Shortly thereafter, Roland found a way to lay her off.

Edwina was relieved when he finally left without asking her to do something for him. It was bad enough to be instructed to send out emails on his behalf. She knew full well that if the message caused a problem, he would announce that she had not understood him, and she was to blame.

However, Roland was also not beyond having her do work for him that had nothing to do with the museum. The week before he had given her a list of names and email addresses to confirm a meeting. Only after he left did she realize from the text that the meeting was to organize a charity concert benefiting his church. This was strictly against museum policy, but if she complained to Human Resources, he would claim that she had volunteered to help him.

She had just turned back to her computer screen when she sensed someone in the doorway. Looking up, she found Roland watching her. Apparently, he had not returned to his office after all.

"You know, Edwina, with the economy the way it is

right now, I can appreciate the difficulty you are having finding a major sponsor for the craft festival."

"It is understandable that the management of Sandstrom Investments is reluctant to participate this year, afraid it will look like wasteful spending given the current economic situation," she reminded him, naming the sponsor for the past three years.

"Such companies don't mind putting their name on a small seminar or being one of many sponsors for an important exhibition, but being a major sponsor for a craft festival is not in their best interest right now." His derogatory tone when he said "craft festival" was not lost on Edwina.

"And The Textile Market is far enough away that things should be looking up by then," she added.

"Well, don't worry if you cannot find a major sponsor, just carry on," Roland said with what she thought was a conspiratorial wink. Something she had never seen him do before.

Had she been more adept at her job, Edwina could have filled the void of one major sponsor with several smaller ones. Her predecessors had developed relationships with a large number of companies and enthusiastically kept them interested in the museum while, at the same time, cultivating new sponsors. Edwina just did not have the type of personality needed to chat up marketing executives and encourage them to support Summerston - something that she desperately needed, especially with the downturn in the economy.

While relieved that Roland would not be expecting miracles, she was curious and a little apprehensive. Either he was setting her up or Adrienne. Or both.

FOURTEEN

As Roland departed Edwina's office, the craft festival contact number was ringing in the Richmond House. A gentleman asked Elinor a series of questions about facilities to entertain guests and advertising opportunities. It soon became apparent that he was interested in more than just a picnic area parking space; so she switched the call to Adrienne.

"You are not going to believe this," cried Adrienne a short time later as she bounded down the stairs and into Elinor's office. She could hardly contain her excitement.

"That was Josh Bentley, president of the state's Automobile Dealers Association. He wants to meet with me to discuss all kinds of cooperative efforts for the festival."

"That's wonderful! Everyone has to drive out here; so it fits," said Elinor.

"I don't know what kind of sponsorship money we are discussing; it sounded more like a number of in-kind arrangements which can be just as lucrative. He mentioned a display of antique cars which will attract a lot of car enthusiasts and putting on events for children with their road safety mascot. He also talked about drawings for free AAA memberships and, perhaps, even getting them involved. It was all very encouraging."

Later, when told of the contact, Edwina shrugged, hiding her annoyance. She told Adrienne she had been trying to reach him for years with no success. Making it sound like it was his fault she had been unable to secure him as a museum sponsor.

This was not the only sponsorship that had materialized without Edwina's help. A few weeks earlier, a friend of one of the festival volunteers, Trevor T. Erskine, III had contacted Adrienne about sponsoring the painted birdhouse silent auction.

Roland had been unimpressed when told of Trevor's offer to help. Roland did not recognize the name, and he had not instructed anyone on his staff to contact Trevor, something that was a matter of form with any new sponsor. For some reason, Roland seemed to think that he did not exist - that Trevor was just a name Adrienne was listing on the program to make the festival look more successful.

FIFTEEN

A week later, when Adrienne had just concluded a meeting with the tent and canopy supplier for the craft festival, her cell phone rang.

Without a greeting, Roland told her she had thirty minutes to review the festival brochure before it would be sent to the printer. As far as he was concerned it was fine. He was on his way to a meeting, but she could pick it up in his office and then contact Rosalind.

Uttering an unlady-like expletive, Adrianne ran upstairs to her office, grabbed her coat and the brochure file. As she raced down the stairs, she yelled to Elinor, "Call Theresa and tell her I won't be able to discuss the flowers with her this afternoon. I was supposed to call her at 2:30. Roland has just given me thirty minutes to review the brochure. I know very well he has been sitting on it. If you need me, I'll be in Rosalind's office. Thanks."

She locked the door on her way out and walked rapidly to her car. It would take her ten minutes to drive to the staff parking area near the museum, reach Roland's office in William's House and then go on to Rosalind's. At a time like this, it was inconvenient to have her office in the historic Richmond House. However, for the most part it was extremely advantageous. Being on the festival grounds, she could easily show vendors, artisans, suppliers and workmen locations and conditions. Plus, being away from the administrative offices also meant she had a certain amount of autonomy, something that greatly irritated Roland.

Last year, he had done something about this, convincing the director that during December the museum should operate a Christmas store in the Richmond House. He argued the location was very accessible, being on a busy major road. Patrons could park next to the building which would encourage them to make more purchases. Shopping in the museum gift shop always involved carrying purchases some distance back to the museum's parking lot. Dr. Kent had agreed, and the shop manager had been delighted. Her sales were down by twenty-five percent, and she needed something to boost the numbers.

While preparing for The Textile Market Adrienne and Elinor had been forced to spend a lot of time packing their office supplies, files and notebooks. A moving firm was hired to transport everything to Williams House. All of the electronic equipment had to be tagged, disassembled and then reassembled by the IT department. Moving to another location and settling into those offices for several months and then, of course, moving everything back again had been extremely disruptive. Exactly what Roland had intended. And, of course, being in the Williams House meant he could drop in to their offices frequently to keep them off balance.

At a departmental meeting just prior to the move, he had made the point of saying to Adrienne, "Once you relocate to the Williams House offices, I can keep an eye on you" - making it sound like they required close supervision. Nothing could be further from the truth because no one in the department worked longer hours or with more dedication than Adrienne and Elinor. But humiliating employees in front of their peers was a frequently used tactic for Roland.

While beneficial to Roland, the replacement of the festival offices with a Christmas store was a financial disaster for the museum. Deluding himself that he was an expert on retail marketing, Roland had also persuaded Dr. Kent that the shop should feature only holiday food gift baskets. Why, he reasoned, order from a catalog or the Internet when you could come to Summerston for your holiday needs. When the figures were tallied, store sales had been dismal. And the museum had the cost of two moves to absorb. Not surprisingly, Roland made it clear that the store manager was at fault, having failed to market the Christmas store properly.

SIXTEEN

The brochure was in an envelope marked "Adrienne" on Roland's desk. She took it to the department's reception area where attractively upholstered wing chairs awaited donors visiting Roland or Dr. Kent. As she reviewed it, she was instantly struck by its muted ecru color. The vibrant colors used for past brochures had been eye-catching, making the photographs stand out. Even the photographs this year were not especially inspiring and featured so many women it looked like a sorority event advertisement. Adrienne was disappointed to find no photos of the exciting new events added to the festival to attract more attention, and both were barely mentioned in the sections describing the festival highlights. In addition, a quick perusal of these sections revealed numerous errors.

Anticipating an unpleasant meeting with Rosalind, Adrienne left Williams House and quickly traversed the short distance to the main museum building. She greeted the security guard and passed into the employee-only section of the building. During the elevator ride to the fifth floor, she had a moment to think about her approach to Rosalind. Never on the best of terms, working with her on this brochure was going to be a real challenge

After receiving a perfunctory greeting from Rosalind, Adrienne cleared a leaning pile of catalogs off a chair and set them next to an equally unstable pile of file folders on a bookcase located near the door. While hardly the neatest person, herself, Adrienne could never understand how Rosalind was able to work amidst such clutter.

"Roland approved the brochure, so it's ready to go," announced Rosalind.

"I'm afraid he missed a couple of things, and I wanted to discuss the design with you," Adrienne responded. "I am curious about the background color choice, and I noticed a textured appearance."

"It's designed to resemble twill. In the spring so many of the museum visitors are wearing it - women's casual jackets, men's slacks. We decided it would be appropriate for the season."

"Very creative," murmured Adrienne. The texture was an interesting concept, but the color looked too dull for this type of brochure. She knew she would not get it changed, so she decided to move on.

She pointed out times and names that were incorrect which Rosalind agreed to change. Then Adrienne raised the issue of so many photographs showing only women.

"Ridiculous," Rosalind retorted. "No one notices any-thing like that - and these were the best photographs."

Adrienne knew the museum photographer had taken hundreds of photographs at the event last year, and there were plenty showing families together and men shopping or selling their art work. Either the ones in this year's bro-chure were specifically selected or the staff was not inclined to spend a lot of time looking for a variety of pictures. Most likely the latter. She also knew that if she did not make too much of an issue now, Rosalind might reconsider and have her staff switch some of the photographs. It had happened often enough in the past for Adrienne to know how to handle this particular concern. Adrienne usually got what she wanted in the end, but Rosalind needed to think any changes were strictly her ideas.

Adrienne turned her attention to the absence of publicity for the new children's activity and the silent auction.

"We would like to promote the two new activities with photographs," she began.

"There's no room for any more photos," Rosalind interrupted her.

"With twenty-three photos in the brochure, I think we could swap out two for the children's Pottery Place and for the painted birdhouse silent auction. We have provided you with several professional photographs for both of them."

Rosalind abruptly turned away, looked at her watch and announced she was late for a meeting. Gathering up several folders she moved away from her desk toward the door and told Adrienne, "I'll get back to you."

Adrienne made her way out of the building, returned to her car and headed down the museum drive. As aggravated as she was with Rosalind, she now needed to put the conversation out of her mind and concentrate on the festival planning meeting tomorrow afternoon.

SEVENTEEN

By noon the next day, Adrienne had firmed up a number of arrangements and given Elinor the agenda for the meeting scheduled at 3:30. This was the first of two formal meetings held at Richmond House prior to the festival to discuss the plans and clarify each museum department's responsibilities.

A late nineteenth century stone building Richmond House had been the residence of a well-to-do farmer, whose property had been purchased by Arthur McAlister. The first floor featured three spacious rooms and a kitchen. A bathroom and three rooms currently used for Adrienne's office and storage were on the second floor.

After lunch Elinor arranged chairs around the large circular table now occupying what had once been a family dining room. With the additional chairs she placed along the walls, the room could accommodate almost everyone. A few people usually ended up sitting in the doorways between rooms, so extra chairs were stacked just inside the door leading to the former living room.

No longer filled with sofas and wing chairs facing the fireplace, it currently housed an extraordinary model of the festival grounds. Created ten years ago by a volunteer, it enabled Adrienne to move miniature tents or vehicles around to demonstrate the layout. Each year, as needed, the volunteer generously created new items.

Elinor finished her preparations by placing agendas and accompanying documents on the round table and beverage bottles and napkins on a long narrow table near the model. Nicki had promised to bring Dining Unlimited's famous oatmeal raisin cookies from the cafeteria. Elinor often wondered if those attending came to be educated or fed.

Around 3:20 museum staff members began arriving until by 3:30 just about everyone was there. As usual, Roland was late and made a grand entrance, requiring someone to get him a chair and everyone to move closer around the table. Just as Adrienne was about to start the meeting, Rosalind, even later, rushed in waving a handful of papers.

"You must look at this now so that my staff can send it to the printer," she called handing them to Adrienne.

"Rosalind, everyone has arrived for the meeting; so we'll have to do this when it is over."

Stony faced, Rosalind went into the adjoining room, took a chair and sat in the doorway, just out of sight of most of those at the table. During much of the meeting she looked angry and distracted, often reading something in her lap and paying little attention to the discussion around her.

Adrienne progressed through the agenda discussing the preview party and event day issues - security, picnic parking procedures, vendors, children's activities, the painted birdhouse silent auction, food and tent locations. Almost everyone participated, and she was pleased with the results.

The only disappointment was Edwina's report. She explained that, thus far, she had been unable to secure a major sponsor. This had never happened before. She vowed to keep trying. Adrienne thought she detected a small smile on Roland's face as Edwina made her announcement.

When the meeting broke up close to 5pm, Rosalind reminded Adrienne that the final version of the brochure had to go to the printer immediately. Adrienne laid it out on the table and noted that most of the errors had been corrected. However, four items in the schedule which had been reversed needed adjusting. And it was still far too dull for her taste. Several of the photographs had been replaced, so there was more balance. To her surprise there was a very poor, amateur photo of one of the birdhouses. It was the photograph submitted by the artist prior to delivery. She knew that the museum photographer had taken perfectly staged photos of the two houses already at the museum. It was also, by far, the smallest photo in the brochure. Almost tiny, in fact, and difficult to see.

"This looks good, but I am concerned about the quality and the size of the birdhouse photograph," she told Rosalind, "and we need to correct the four errors I have circled."

"The photo is okay," Rosalind snapped. "We preferred the side view on that one."

Roland, who had remained behind, watched this interplay with a poker face.

"It looks very amateurish with the artist's fireplace in the background. It is not the same high quality as the other photos you are using," Adrienne replied.

Rosalind went into Elinor's office at the rear of the

building, picked up the phone and punched in an extension in her department.

"We need to make some changes to the festival brochure. Bring it up on your computer," she ordered her employee.

"I don't care if you do have a doctor's appointment. You will stay until this is finished."

Rosalind read off the changes Adrienne had circled. "Make those changes and email it to me at Elinor Pierson's computer," she said and hung up.

No mention had been made of the tiny birdhouse photo. And Roland had not intervened on Adrienne's behalf.

For the next five minutes Roland, Adrienne and Rosalind made small talk with Roland doing most of the talking, complaining about his sister-in-law. By the time the anticipated email arrived, Adrienne was feeling a great deal of sympathy for the much maligned woman, no matter how irritating she might be in reality.

Elinor printed out the brochure and placed it on her desk. Everyone looked at it, and it was approved. To Adrienne, however, it was one of the least successful she had seen in the many years she had worked on the festival.

Two days later, she received the final version from the staff member charged with its production. With a wry smile, she noticed that the amateur birdhouse photo had been replaced. While still small, it was the professional photograph.

EIGHTEEN

The next six weeks passed quickly with, to Adrienne's relief, little interference from Roland. However, his apparent acquiescence to her arrangements did not, necessarily, mean he actually approved of what she was doing.

Wrapping up the final details for the preview party, Adrienne spoke at length with her friend Theresa Redding about the table flower arrangements. Theresa, a close friend, was a very successful stock broker who also had a reputation as a creative flower designer. Friends called her to do arrangements and decorations for dinner parties, high school proms and even for funerals. She was always most generous with her time and charged only for the flowers and containers.

"I thought we could do something to tie in with the new weathervane exhibition at the museum," Adrienne suggested. "It would promote it, especially if we place some advertising next to the arrangements."

"That sounds like a great idea. Are there any particular designs being featured, or does it cover everything?" Theresa asked.

"The title is *From Soaring Eagles to Strutting Roosters*

- 19th century *Weathervanes*, so the emphasis is on the use of birds," Adrienne explained.

"Let me check around and see what I can find. We could always use Philadelphia Eagles mugs," Theresa joked.

Adrienne laughed and disconnected. She knew whatever Theresa came up with would be most appropriate. Unlike last year, when the museum's head flower designer, Patricia Holester, had selected pumpkin shaped containers. They had been purchased several years before and used for a fall symposium dinner. Not only were they inappropriate for an event in the spring, they should not have been billed to the festival. The department sponsoring the symposium had already paid for the containers. By passing the cost on to the festival, Patricia's department was reimbursed twice while the festival expenses were unnecessarily increased.

With her orders to trim the budget, Adrienne was not going to allow the festival to be overcharged again. The festival executive committee had been very pleased with her reducing the flower budget by over two thousand dollars while still maintaining the quality of the arrangements.

She wondered if Roland would encourage Thurston to challenge her decision not to use the museum's floral designers. Using them would, of course, enhance the revenue figures for Thurston's department. For that very reason, his assistant and Patricia's boss, James Grover was promoting an exclusive use policy for events at the museum. Anyone holding an event requiring flowers would have to use the museum's floral designers.

Naturally, Roland would not raise this issue, himself. Especially after he had agreed in front of the committee members that Theresa should be asked to do the flowers.

NINETEEN

fter talking with Theresa, Adrienne left her office
and went downstairs to confer with Elinor. As she
passed by the door to the front room she greeted
three ladies who were filling ticket orders for the festival.

In the late fall, two volunteers had begun helping with
the festival. Kate Charles and her friend, Susan Penn,
had been joined in February by Serena Fields. Kate and
Serena had volunteered together at the museum for many
years, and with Susan the three of them made a good
team. They especially enjoyed the relaxed atmosphere at
Richmond House. Adrienne respected their talents and
encouraged their initiative. They assembled packets for
those purchasing picnic parking spots and for the vendors,
filed material in festival notebooks, delivered advertising
materials and helped Elinor with copying. Adrienne also
asked them to take charge of the painted birdhouse silent
auction and to help her with the "Pottery Place".

For the auction they contacted a large number of local
artists asking them to paint a wooden birdhouse supplied
by the festival. To their delight twenty artists, including
a nationally recognized folk artist from Portland, Maine,
accepted the invitation. The silent auction would be held
during the festival. Since each year the festival drew a

large, enthusiastic crowd of close to 25,000 people, it was hoped that this new event would be very profitable.

With many well-known local artists involved and a totally new concept for the festival, it was assumed the auction would provide an excellent publicity opportunity. Especially so because no other charity in the area had used the idea.

Rosalind told Adrienne to submit information to her, and the volunteers put together a notebook containing everything the publicity department needed. The notebook was delivered to Rosalind in early January.

As time went on it became apparent that the auction would receive scant publicity. Rosalind informed Adrienne that the area magazines and newspapers were not interested in it. Adrienne found this very hard to believe. One of the newspaper reporters routinely authored articles about Summerston, and it seemed anything the museum wanted publicized appeared in the paper. The upcoming weathervane exhibition, for example, would be highlighted with two full pages in *Local Happenings*. And it had already been featured in an article about collecting for investment in the financial section.

The publicity department regularly wined and dined the features editor of the local monthly magazine. She was always looking for something original to highlight. In the past her articles featured entertaining interviews with a variety of vendors. However, this year her story on the festival would consist of five lines of text and a 3/4 page photograph of a potter who was not returning to this year's event. Clearly something was not right.

Even if other outlets would not publicize it, certainly in-house publications could highlight the auction. But there had been nothing about the auction in the first festival publicity piece, and Adrienne was keenly aware of how hard she had to fight to get a decent photograph in the brochure.

For the first time the museum's email list was being used to promote the festival. Adrienne sent Roland an email request to focus on the auction in the first April "email blast." Roland rarely responded to emails preferring not to put things in writing and often ignored messages all together. So she was not surprised when he did not respond. However, she did receive a response from Tina in the publicity department. She informed Adrienne that Roland and James Grover were overseeing the festival's publicity, and they felt that the auction was only one small piece of the festival and should be publicized as a part of the whole.

"Well, at least that confirms our suspicions," Adrienne told Elinor and the volunteers. "Roland is definitely directing what Rosalind does."

"Sounds a lot like sabotage to me," remarked Susan.

"But where does James fit into this?" asked Serena. "Why would he have any say about publicity for the festival?"

"Publicity comes under Tours and Education, so perhaps Thurston has Rosalind reporting to his assistant, James. Thurston is away so much, he may have given him that responsibility," suggested Elinor. "I'm sure it's no coincidence that you frequently see Roland, Thurston and James together at lunch - usually with Dr. Kent."

"It is very discouraging. We have been getting emails and telephone calls from a number of the artists, concerned about the lack of publicity. Because most of them do their own PR, they know what is involved and what should be done. Some of them have listed the festival and put photos of their birdhouses on their own websites. One of the out-of-state artists, on her own, sent a photo of her birdhouse to her local paper and make the front page. They cannot believe Summerston cannot get any publicity." Kate was clearly annoyed.

"We are doing some small things ourselves, but what is really needed is a major article. Let's hope a week or so before the preview there is a large spread in the paper," said Serena.

"How do the curators always get such great publicity for the exhibitions?" Kate asked.

"For one thing, the director and Roland are all for special exhibitions. The Board of Trustees is full of collectors who would, undoubtedly, be concerned if they did not see adequate publicity for an exhibition. And second, we all know Dr. Kent and Roland would like to put an end to the festival. They have made no secret of that." Adrienne was quite adamant.

"By sabotaging the publicity for the auction, fewer people will know about it and come to bid. That will keep the bids low and the profits down for the festival. Then Roland can point to it's poor showing and pronounce the auction a failure. This will cast doubt on the future of the festival and its planner. He can say my ideas don't work, and the festival is growing stale. Time for something new - as in a new planner and a new event."

"Does he have something in mind?" asked Kate

"I am not sure. We know that Roland has invited an event planner to be his guest at the preview and the festival. The planner is an old friend of Nicki's; so I have to think they are in cahoots. And I know that he would like to get rid of me. He cannot do it openly, but if he makes things too uncomfortable, he figures I will quit."

"Why didn't he just lay you off during the last round of cuts?" asked Serena.

"Elinor and I have both been at Summerston too long. If they lay us off, it will be costly in terms of severance and benefits, but if we quit, it doesn't cost them."

"This is really ugly. He is using these very talented artists who have generously donated their time to get at you and to get rid of the festival." Susan could not believe someone would do such a thing.

"And unfortunately, the artists are not the only ones being harmed," said Adrienne and Elinor almost simultaneously.

"Corinne Ralston from the Pottery Palace has been working with us for almost a year to set up The Pottery Place where children can paint and decorate items for their parents. It is such a cute idea, and she is donating all of the materials - little plates, bowls, vases, those types of things. She has paints, glitter, stickers, lots of fun materials. Rosalind hasn't give her any significant publicity, either. The Pottery Place did not even get a photo in the brochure. Needless to say, Corinne is rather upset," Adrienne explained.

TWENTY

The first week in April, everyone gathered at Richmond House for the final departmental staff meeting. While the lack of a major sponsor was still disappointing and Rosalind's terse publicity report proved uninformative, progress made by other departments was encouraging. On the whole, Adrienne was pleased. The last item on the agenda was the preview party.

A few minutes into Adrienne's presentation, James Grover questioned the use of an outside flower designer.

Prepared for his question, Adrienne explained, "Last year the flowers, arranged by the museum designers, cost almost $3000, so the festival executive committee agreed to use an outside designer who is volunteering her time and will charge only $700 - the cost of materials."

Elinor handed Adrienne two containers, one featuring roosters and the other an eagle motif.

"Theresa found these for a very reasonable price. To encourage people to visit the weathervane exhibition, we will place advertising tent cards next to the flower arrangement on each table."

Most of those around the table expressed interest and approval. Roland and James were not among them.

The meeting ended on time, and as they put chairs

away Adrienne and Elinor discussed several issues they needed to address as well as James' comments. "I was surprised that James did not make more of an issue about the flowers."

"You handled that very well," Elinor complimented Adrienne. "And Theresa will be delighted with the response to her containers."

Several days later, Adrienne received a call from Theresa. She was at her supplier preparing to order the flowers. Adrienne approved of her selection and had just hung up when Roland called.

"I have been talking to James, and we cannot slight Patricia. She is to do the flowers."

Adrienne could hardly respond, she was so furious. "The containers have been purchased, and Theresa has ordered the flowers this morning."

"Cancel the flowers, and I am sure you can return those containers."

"You know the committee has set a $700 budget. Can Patricia stay within that?"

There was a slight hesitation on the other end, as if Roland was deciding whether or not to argue the point. "Call her and make the arrangements," he said and disconnected.

TWENTY-ONE

A pril 9, the day of the preview party for *From Soaring Eagles to Strutting Roosters - 19th century Weathervanes*, was warm but overcast. As soon as the museum closed, dining services and museum staff members moved in to create a festive party atmosphere in the reception area. The curators took one last walk through their exhibition, relieved that after two years of planning it would finally make its debut. By 6:30 everything was in place, and the doors opened to admit the first patrons.

The forecast of showers had proven accurate, and a light rain fell on those waiting to enter the brightly lit reception area. As usual, Julia had not seen the pitfalls of having only one large table for the name tags. Letitia, Cora and two volunteers were doing the best they could, but the logistics were defeating them. Frequently in each other's way, it was taking too long for those standing in the rain. Roland had foreseen the problem when he reviewed her plan but had decided not to mention it. Better that she look incompetent and flustered in front of the director and board members. Should anyone question his oversight, he had but to say that she had assured him it would work. And Dr. Kent was all about managers taking the initiative - more like all about letting them take the blame. For her part, Julia was directing people to the table and getting the tags for those she recognized. Edwina and several of her colleagues were also picking up tags and taking them to patrons as they divested themselves of rain coats and umbrellas in the cloak room. Unfortunately, this only added to the confusion.

Standing under a blue striped umbrella outside the museum, Judith Jordan and her son, Stewart, watched the line inch toward the reception area entrance. With her short styled salt and pepper hair, non-descript rain coat and mulberry sheath dress, she was unremarkable, someone you would easily overlook. And that was just the way she liked it. Stewart, a handsome man in his early forties, on the other hand, stood out with his elegantly tailored suit, regimental tie and crisp white shirt. He could easily be mistaken for an ambassador. And not only in his appearance but in his diplomatic demeanor. Outgoing and friendly on social occasions, he was an intelligent and tactful negotiator in business. But when it suited him, he could also, as they say, play the fool. Those who underestimated either one of them did so at their peril.

"They are certainly running true to form this evening," Judith spoke quietly so only Stewart could hear. "Why we have to wear name tags around our necks at these things is beyond me. It's a party not a Rotary convention." She was more amused than annoyed. Unlike some of those around them who were now quite vocally expressing their contempt.

"I suspect it's because the staff cannot remember who the major donors are and don't want to embarrass themselves."

"As if keeping said donors standing in the rain isn't

embarrassment enough! How hard is it simply to be nice to everyone."

Eventually, they reached the doors and were rewarded with an enthusiastic welcome from Edwina who had met them at earlier previews. That is Stewart received such a greeting. Judith was acknowledged but just barely.

Standing off to the side of the large room, Thurston and Roland sipped glasses of chilled white wine and made unflattering comments about the guests.

"I see Mrs. Jordan is her usual ravishing self this evening in an off-the-rack ten year old gown," sneered Thurston.

"And escorted by her air head son. Nice suit, but that's about it."

"Oh, I don't know," observed Thurston. "He is one handsome man - never married, either. I wonder...."

Roland's attention was drawn to a petite blond young woman escorted by a scruffy looking bearded man in a leather jacket and jeans. "Uh, oh this could get interesting. I saw her sister come in a few minutes ago."

Following his glance, Thurston shuddered. "I remember the shouting match they got into at the last preview. We had to call Security. And one of them was forbidden to use the golf club facilities for six months after their last blow-up there. Why do we keep inviting them - and more to the point why do they keep coming to previews. It cannot be to enjoy the exhibitions."

"Unfortunately, they are the heirs to a sizeable fortune; so we have to cultivate them," said Roland. "And they only come to show each other up. I'll go tell Edwina to be sure to keep them apart."

Seeing Roland with Thurston lurking in a corner

making fun of people did not surprise Roland's staff. This was their standard behavior at such functions. Only when Dr. Kent put in an appearance did they develop a sudden urge to socialize.

Not one to mingle himself, Dr. Kent stood imperiously in the center of the room and let others seek him out. Not that there was an absence of people willing to do so. He knew how to flatter the right people. Such benevolence, however, was only reserved for the very wealthy, and he gave scant attention to anyone else.

Watching his performance, Judith and Stewart exchanged amused glances. They had also observed Roland and Thurston and found their behavior humorous as well.

"Arthur and Andrew McAlister must be turning over in their graves," said Judith. "They would never tolerate such arrogance."

"It is amusing to watch, but sad at the same time. No finesse, no class. I don't understand how most of these people don't see how phony they are."

Nodding in agreement, Judith approached the double doors for the East Gallery, site of the weathervane exhibition.

"Let's go see the weathervanes and afterwards we can let Thurston and Roland fawn all over us - or you, at least. I think Thurston fancies you," Judith laughed.

Giving his mother a "you can't be serious" look, Stewart held open one of the doors and followed her into the exhibition.

Later, on the way home, Stewart admonished her. "You really ought to be ashamed of yourself," he laughed. "Actually, you should get an Academy Award."

"It's fun," she replied. Pretending to be just his mother, an unsophisticated, vague woman who now appeared slightly senile, had become a well perfected act. And a role she thoroughly enjoyed, especially when she eventually did step out of that character and, as Stewart put it, pulled the trigger.

TWENTY-TWO

Discussing the past evening's preview, two curators responsible for *From Soaring Eagles to Strutting Roosters - 19th century Weathervanes* made their way to the exhibition galleries. One was due to present a tour to a group of museum members, and her companion wanted to observe in preparation for her own tour later in the day.

"Did you talk with Mrs. Jordan and her son last night?" one asked the other.

"Yes, they made a point of finding me and offering congratulations. They are always so encouraging and complimentary. Interested in me as a person."

"Same thing with me. It is such a pleasure to see them. But I have noticed that they don't really mingle and seem to be watching Thurston, Roland and Dr. Kent. Somehow I get the impression they are not quite what they appear. Not that they are phony or anything like that, just that there is more than meets the eye."

"I know what you mean. According to my aunt, Mrs. Jordan is related to the McAlister family but never mentions it. It is almost as if she is looking out for their interests without Dr. Kent and company realizing it. My aunt is pretty sure no one in the administration knows her as anything but a donor through her family foundation."

"I like the idea of someone surreptitiously watching that crowd. We are very fortunate to have the boss we do. I don't know how those people stand working for Roland and Thurston."

"Agreed. Uh, oh speak of the devil or devils, here comes the dynamic duo."

As the curators greeted a group of members at the entrance to the exhibition, Thurston and Roland passed them. And, as usual, they appeared engrossed in their conversation and acknowledged no one. Hardly the behavior their hired consultants recommended to staff responsible for museum visitor and member satisfaction.

TWENTY-THREE

E lsewhere in the museum building, others were also discussing the weathervane exhibition preview but for different reasons. Dr. Alfred Jackson, Museum Librarian, and several of the curators were meeting with their boss Jeremy Aycres. A year ago the library had received a remarkable collection of letters relating to the Garges family of Doylestown, PA. Because the festival was featuring an appliquéd bed cover created by Sarah Ann Garges, the curators had decided to use the letters as the basis for a one act play. Students from the Leland University drama department would perform the play during the craft festival preview.

Six months ago when Jeremy and Alfred suggested the play, Adrienne was thrilled. The festival preview was going to be one museum party no one was likely to forget.

Alfred was delighted with the play and wanted to share his enthusiasm with Jeremy. Everyone involved with the project was anxious to change the all too predictable nature of the museum's previews and offer something entirely different. There had been no compliments for the previous evening's reception - except for the strawberries dipped in chocolate which everyone agreed were addictive.

Dr. Kent had originally objected to a play, voicing the concern that it would not be sophisticated enough for those attending the preview. He made it sound as if they were putting on a puppet show with a cardboard box stage, make-shift curtain and sock puppets. Both Alfred and Jeremy had been insulted and annoyed. Jeremy had already sounded out several museum trustees and received enthusiastic approval. It seemed only Dr. Kent preferred the staid, boring preview receptions. Perhaps, he feared any entertainment would divert attention away from him.

Eventually he had acquiesced, probably hoping the play would be a failure. That, however, was unlikely given the highly-respected reputation of Leland's drama department. Its productions were always sold out months in advance.

After complimenting the authors, Jeremy enjoyed reviewing the costume selections with his staff. Leland would secure the costumes once the choices were made. There was a lot of good natured kidding about whether or not Alfred and Jeremy as well as the curators would be expected to don 19th century period dress.

As he left the meeting, Alfred reflected on what a pleasure it was to work with Jeremy. His office door and his mind were always open to his staff and any suggestions they might make. Nothing was considered too trivial to discuss. Everyone in the department looked forward to the monthly staff meetings. While they dealt with some very serious issues, Jeremy made the meetings not only interesting but fun. He also provided delectable home made pastries or cookies - his wife was a superb cook. And, sometimes, he wore a wizard's hat or some other piece of apparel appropriate for the occasion. While such behavior was considered childish by Roland and Thurston, Jeremy's staff appreciated it. Not one person had left the department since Jeremy became associate director.

Getting along with people and enjoying his work came naturally to Jeremy. Born in New Hampshire to parents who were never reluctant to show affection toward their children, who encouraged them in their endeavors and who supported their aspirations, he described his childhood as more *Leave It to Beaver* than reality show. His father was a well-known author and tenured professor at Dartmouth College. Dr. Aycres made light of departmental squabbles and was known as someone who could bring opposing views together with respect and humor. Jeremy's mother worked part-time as a librarian, but was always there for him and his younger sister. She was his Cub Scout den mother, his sister's Brownie leader and helped at their school. Both parents attended their school plays or athletic events - his father had even taken one of his classes to Jeremy's soccer match the day his team won their division play-offs.

After receiving his Master's degree from Dartmouth in Art History with a specialty in Folk Art, Jeremy taught for several years at a small private college. He found the students stimulating but the politics of academia too stressful. He couldn't say that his father had not warned him. Several curatorial positions at museums in upper state New York followed. The work was both interesting and tedious, but the tedium was relieved by another young curator who was enchanting. Shortly after they were married, a family friend contacted Jeremy about an opening at

Summerston. With the friend's strong recommendation in hand, Jeremy applied for the job and was hired.

It did not hurt that the family friend was Associate Director of Tours and Education at the museum. He became Jeremy's mentor and taught him, mostly by example, how to be a successful manager. A few months before this universally respected and well-liked administrator retired, he proudly applauded Jeremy's elevation to Associate Director of Research. From his retirement home on the west coast of Florida he continued to support him, reminding Jeremy to always be true to himself. Both were dismayed as the likes of first Thurston and then Roland joined the museum staff. But Jeremy's devotion to Summerston and the encouragement of his mentor kept him at the museum, to be a voice for the McAlisters' values.

TWENTY-FOUR

hile Jeremy amused his staff with speculation about period costumes, things were far more serious at Richmond House. Elinor was trying to calm an irritated caller - the seventh one in two days. After promising to look into the matter and call right back, she hung up and went upstairs to talk with Adrienne.

"Mrs. Thompson just called and, like all of the others, wanted to know why she had not received her invitation to the festival preview."

"She has been a mainstay and one of our biggest supporters - never misses one," said Adrienne.

"According to Edwina, the invitations went out almost two weeks ago. I could understand it if the same zip code was involved, but they all live in different places," noted Elinor.

"Let me call Edwina and see what list she used. It should have been the edited one from last year, as I requested."

But once Adrienne got through to Edwina, she remained unenlightened. Edwina could not remember exactly what she had told Jenny who did the computer work to compile mailing lists. And she was unable to find a copy of the formal request she had sent to her. But Edwina was sure she had requested the names Adrienne wanted. And, she added, Roland had approved the request.

Adrienne also tried to reach Jenny, only to learn that she was out of the office for two days.

Shortly after her return to work, Jenny emailed Adrienne the list she had compiled. Adrienne was astonished. How Edwina could have selected those particular groups of people was beyond belief. She wondered if it had been incompetence or something more sinister. But it certainly explained why so few acceptances had been received for the preview.

Within a few days, with the help of volunteers and a sympathetic printer, five hundred invitations were in the mail to many of those who should have been on the original list. The mailing should have gone to three times that many, but it was the best they could do given the time constraints.

For the next two weeks acceptances arrived; and five days before the preview Adrienne ordered the hospitality tent based upon that number.

Edwina, however, did not respect the deadline and continued to take acceptances which increased the number beyond the tent's capacity.

"Everyone is not, necessarily, in the hospitality tent at the same time. They go to the other tents to visit the booths or watch the demonstrations," she shrugged as she gave the final numbers to Adrienne two days before the event and after the tent had been installed. The idea that important donors might be uncomfortable in an overcrowded tent did not seem to bother her.

Even with the last minute acceptances, however, the number was still half as many as they had originally anticipated and upon which Dining Unlimited had based its estimated costs. Use of the wrong mailing list had taken its toll.

TWENTY-FIVE

I n spite of such set-backs, or sabotage as Adrienne now thought of it, the Summerston Craft Festival was about to open. Five large, shiny white tents sporting yellow and white striped pennants would be joined tomorrow by rows of cars whose owners had prepared gourmet picnics. Attractively positioned around the exterior of the tents, brightly colored flowers and potted trees lent a festive air. Artisans had been busy all day unpacking their vetted crafts. Booths within the tents were now ready for those attending the preview.

In the Hospitality Tent, Edwina and her co-workers were putting out name tags and programs. Two long tables, covered by yellow flowered cloths, had been installed at the entrance where the staff would greet guests. Susan, Serena and Kate arrived with name tags for the birdhouse artists who were to be the museum's special guests that evening. Each artist's tag featured a photograph of the particular house painted by that artist. Plans called for the volunteers to use part of the second table. Edwina, however, had no intention of sharing.

"Just find any table to set up on," she told them, gesturing to the tall, round yellow cloth-covered cocktail tables each sporting a flower arrangement in the center. She turned her back to them and continued with her task.

Exchanging bemused glances, they selected a table close to the entrance and laid out the name tags and small gifts they had purchased to thank the artists.

Ten minutes before seven, Roland and Thurston entered the tent to check on the preparations. As usual, they were stylishly dressed in perfectly pressed slacks and linen sport jackets, white shirts and their standard bow ties - navy blue with red stripes for Roland and bright green with yellow polka dots for Thurston. Barely acknowledging the volunteers who greeted them, they took a quick look at the guest list Edwina produced and mentally noted those whom Dr. Kent needed to greet. They offered no assistance to their hard-working staff and, instead, strode around the tent with a patrician air, sampling hors d'oeuvres.

Guests began to arrive, among them one of the artists. No name tag was found when she announced herself.

"I painted one of the birdhouses for the silent auction," explained the attractive gray-haired lady dressed in a striking mauve suit with a white silk blouse and on the arm of a distinguished looking man in a navy blue sport jacket and tan slacks.

"Oh," said an unsmiling Edwina, "Your name tags are over there." She pointed to her right as she called an enthusiastic welcome to a man standing behind them.

Having observed this exchange, Serena quickly approached the couple and greeted them warmly, trying to compensate for Edwina's rude behavior. Kate and Susan decided that, despite the previous instructions, they would stand next to the long tables at the entrance and intercept the artists to avoid more unpleasantness.

As the evening progressed, Edwina and her colleagues as well as Dr. Kent and Roland completely ignored the artists. Apparently, they did not feel their contribution to the festival was substantial enough to warrant their being treated as honored guests. Or they intended to embarrass Adrienne by their rude treatment of the artists and thus damage the reputation of the festival. Blinded by their own arrogance, they failed to realize how badly their behavior reflected on the museum.

The volunteers made up for the lack of attention by introducing the artists to other senior staff members and to their fellow guests. Serena, Kate and Susan made sure that they had what they wanted to eat and drink and directed them to the tents housing sale booths and special demonstrations. Everyone was reminded not to miss the play scheduled for 7:30 in the adjoining tent.

Unfortunately, as they made their way to the performance, several of the artists overheard Roland complaining to Edwina. "We should never have permitted them to attend the preview. Did you see the way that one woman was dressed - gaudy long skirt, looked like a gypsy. The other guests should not be subjected to such people." He continued along the same vein for several minutes before moving toward the entrance of the tent to greet a particularly affluent donor who had just arrived.

The highly respected artist, to whom he referred, was wearing an original Oscar da la Renta ruffled silk blouse and sequined, multi-colored tulle skirt from Neiman Marcus.

TWENTY-SIX

As predicted, after midnight a low pressure system moved in and festival goers had to contend with steady rain during much of the next day. Many of those who had purchased advance tickets for picnic parking spaces put up small canopies and braved the weather. Most picnics were not as elaborate as usual, but the Best of the Fest judges still had a sufficient number of creative entries to make selecting a winner challenging. Eventually, a table with dishes artfully arranged to resemble the pattern of a quilt in the collection was awarded the coveted hand-painted ceramic platter and bragging rights for the host and hostess.

Although advance ticket sales would help the bottom line, the weather definitely affected the actual attendance. Fortunately, most artisans made enough sales or contacts for future orders to be satisfied with the day. But the smaller than anticipated crowd meant the birdhouse silent auction did not attract as much attention as anticipated. The advanced bidding option, designed to compensate for this, was a complete failure due to a lack of publicity.

In the morning Roland, accompanied by Thurston and James, had put in an appearance at the festival. Most of the museum staff members who were manning booths, helping to carry purchases or directing traffic had come in slickers and boots. Roland, a picture of sartorial elegance, appeared in a Brooks Brothers khaki rain coat and matching hat, L.L. Bean rain shoes and carried a plaid Burberry umbrella. The others were similarly attired, looking as though they were attending an afternoon at the opera rather than a craft festival held under tents in a field.

Making clearly audible sarcastic comments, they wandered among the booths but bypassed the lectures and demonstrations presented by renowned local artisans. When they arrived at the silent auction tent, a smiling, friendly couple greeted them and encouraged them to bid on the birdhouses. The response was frosty with Roland pushing past them as if they were not there. His companions looked at the two as if they had just suggested something unseemly and followed him.

After spending less than five minutes in the tent, they strode out and boarded the shuttle to the museum having parked their cars in the paved staff parking area rather than on the festival grounds like everyone else.

At 4pm bidding for the birdhouses closed and volunteers gathered up the bidding sheets. A large results poster was prepared, and as the volunteers straightened it on an easel at the entrance to the tent, Rosalind Pepper appeared. She resembled a giant bumble bee in her hooded yellow rain jacket, matching pants and black boots. With a forced smile, she approached the men adjusting the poster and observed, "You must have had a very successful day."

Overhearing her comment, Susan Penn and her husband joined the group that had gathered to read the auction results. She made a point of calling Rosalind by name and being sure everyone knew that Rosalind was responsible for publicity at the museum before calmly replying, "With almost no publicity, the auction did not go as well as the artists had hoped."

"What do you mean no publicity? I had photographers from the local newspapers in the tent all morning," snapped Rosalind. "You'll get great coverage tomorrow and again next week in the community newspaper."

"Publicity after an auction is hardly helpful," replied an amazed Serena as she walked up to the others standing at the entrance. Everyone exchanged astonished glances. No one could believe that a professional publicity manager could say something quite that ridiculous.

"You have no idea how hard I have been working, no idea at all," yelled Rosalind as she turned and walked away.

"But, indeed, we do," Susan called after her. *As in working against the auction.*

"Thanks a lot," came the angry, shouted reply as Rosalind disappeared around the side of the tent.

"Uh, oh," said Serena shaking her head. "I can just imagine the version of that exchange that will get back to Roland."

In her wildest imagination, she could not have predicted the repercussions.

TWENTY-SEVEN

During the next week, Adrienne did not hear anything from either Roland or Dr. Kent. It was as if this year's festival had never occurred. While the former director had been quite difficult and short on compliments, he had, at least, congratulated staff members by email or telephone after major events. Adrienne sent out her own email thanking everyone at the museum for their support, but still she heard nothing, herself. It was very disheartening.

Serena, Kate and Susan were sympathetic to Adrienne but, at the same time, had their own reasons for being discouraged. They met with her at Richmond House to discuss their concerns about the lack of publicity for the silent auction. Having recruited the artists to participate, they felt responsible for them. They knew the artists had been disappointed with the results of the auction, and the three wanted to do something about it. Adrienne knew that any complaints from her would fall on deaf ears.

After talking with Adrienne, they gathered at Serena's home to decide what they should do. It was agreed that whatever it was, it would be something undertaken only by them. Adrienne was not to be involved. They did not want to cause her any more problems.

"I have known Dr. Kent for a number of years through my association with the hospital auxiliary," said Susan. She and her husband were Leland University alumnae and donors to both the school and the medical center. During his tenure as president they had frequently attended hospital events where Dr. Kent was present. He did not consider their donations significant enough to merit special attention, but she felt he did know who she was.

"Let me call him and set up an appointment for us to discuss our concerns with the way the lack of publicity affected the auction," she suggested to the others. "Having the artists unhappy with the museum is not good PR. I am sure he will be willing to listen, if nothing else."

Taking out her cell phone, she called his office. When no one answered, she left him a voice message.

Several days later Susan called Serena and Kate to tell them that Dr. Kent's secretary had called her. He would not meet with them. Roland was the department head responsible for the festival, so any concerns should be addressed to him.

"Technically, he is correct because contacting Dr. Kent is going behind Roland's back," said Kate.

"True in some ways," responded Serena. "However, our concern is with the public relations department which is not overseen by Roland. And I have always found you often only get results by going to the top. Besides, in this case, Roland is part of the problem."

"Unfortunately, I suspect Dr. Kent may be another part," quipped Kate.

"Susan, you've written reports for the different committees you've chaired, will you put together a report detailing the lack of publicity for the auction?" asked Serena. "I don't mind writing the cover letter to Dr. Kent."

"I appreciate the vote of confidence," Susan said with a smile. "I'll email you two what I come up with, and you can send me your thoughts about it."

"I'll do the same with the letter," added Serena.

Several days later, everyone agreed to the wording of the letter and report, signed the letter, and Susan mailed them to Dr. Kent.

Susan received an almost immediate response - a response that was not only insulting to the three volunteers but to the artists. The letter was sent out under his signature, but the ladies were quite sure it had been written not by Dr. Kent but by Roland. They were appalled by its tone and its content.

But not as appalled as Adrienne was to be when she went to Roland's office for her previously scheduled bi-weekly meeting.

She had already left for her meeting when the three volunteers arrived at the Richmond House to help Elinor prepare a mailing to the festival artisans.

When Adrienne returned half an hour later, she was shaking and collapsed into a chair.

"You are not going to believe what just happened to me," she said fighting back tears.

"Good grief, did you have an accident on the way back?" asked a very concerned Elinor.

"No, nothing like that. It was Roland. He was totally out of control and shouting at me. I was really frightened."

She explained that he told her he did not wish to discuss the festival until their next meeting. He then began yelling about a letter, the volunteers insulting him and other staff members and their being renegades who needed to be kept in check. When she asked him what letter he was talking about, he yelled even louder and refused to show it to her. She remembered the volunteers were going to write to Dr. Kent but could not believe any letter from them would stir up such a violent reaction from Roland. She was so upset that she missed some of what he said but finally asked him what she was supposed to do. He practically screamed at her that she should just be a supervisor and do something about her "damn" volunteers.

She gathered up her papers and left his office, but she was shaking so hard she could not face the steep, open staircase to the first floor. Instead, holding tightly to the banister, she climbed the three stairs to the next level and walked to the back of the building. By the time she reached the end of the hall, she was more under control and able to navigate the enclosed back stairway and leave Williams House through the rear door.

TWENTY-EIGHT

Her listeners were astonished. Roland's reaction was completely irrational. Like the earlier response signed by Dr. Kent, it was "over the top" in relation to the carefully phrased, evidence-based report and letter they had prepared.

Toward the end of the day, Adrienne received a terse email from Roland. "It's not the letter but the outrageous behavior," he wrote.

Printing out a copy, she brought it downstairs to show Serena, Kate and Susan who were still working with Elinor on the mailing.

"If it was the so called 'outrageous behavior' and not the letter, why was nothing said about our 'behavior' immediately after the festival?" Serena wondered.

"It does seem like too much of a coincidence that he would fly off the handle only after the letter was received by Dr. Kent," responded Kate.

"And he suddenly realized that if he criticized the letter it would look like Dr. Kent did not accept constructive criticism - something he claimed to welcome when he took over," said Susan.

"Of course, Dr. Kent's response to us has already

proven just how much he welcomes constructive criticism!" observed Kate.

Voicing the volunteers' earlier conclusion, Adrienne noted, "I would be very surprised to learn that Dr. Kent actually wrote that response. The letter sounded too much like Roland."

"And we know Dr. Kent rarely does anything but edit letters written by staff members," added Elinor.

"Personally, I don't care who wrote it. Dr. Kent signed it, and it was insulting," fumed Serena. "Talk about something being outrageous!"

"Not to mention Roland now accusing us of something we did not do," said Kate. "And we have the witnesses to prove we behaved in a civilized manner."

All three voiced their concerns about Adrienne and how badly she had been treated. They had every right to express their opinions and let Dr. Kent know that donors to the museum, the birdhouse artists, had not been fairly treated. The fact that they had done so should not reflect on Adrienne. Nor should they be maligned for writing to him.

They discussed how Adrienne should proceed, and she finally decided to consult the head of Human Resources - ask for his advice on how to handle the situation. Adrienne was especially concerned that Roland had so blatantly lied about what happened at the festival.

TWENTY-NINE

A drienne was somewhat reluctant to consult Emory Beyer, the head of Human Resources. His department had a less than stellar reputation when it came to discretion. One of his assistants was the wife of a Summerston division manager who knew more about personnel matters than he should have. Adrienne had heard of one instance in which the manager had hinted to a curator that he was aware of the details of a very private conversation between the curator and Emory. The curator had been mortified and then even more upset when the manager winked at him and made snide comments every time they encountered each other. The curator spoke to Emory about it, but nothing happened to alleviate the situation. The curator, eventually, resigned.

In spite of her reluctance, Adrienne knew she needed to follow procedures which meant consulting with Emory on any personnel matters. She made an appointment for first thing Monday morning.

When she met with him, Adrienne discovered that Emory was acquainted with both Susan Penn and Kate Charles. Over the years they had all served together on the parents' association at their children's school. He seemed surprised that Roland would complain about them. He had always been impressed with their leadership and diplomacy as chairmen of various committees and of the association, itself. He had met Serena on several occasions, and she had made a most favorable impression. He listened somewhat sympathetically to Adrienne, but then told her that she needed to consult with Jean Howard, Manager of Volunteers. She was ultimately responsible for all matters involving the museum's volunteers.

Adrienne thanked him for his advice, left the office and started down the hall toward Jean's office. A notice on the hall bulletin board caught her eye, and she stopped for a moment to read it. As she did, she saw Roland coming in the side door and disappearing around the corner toward Emory's office. *Interesting*, she thought. *I cannot imagine his appearance is a coincidence.*

When she reached the door to Jean's office, she noticed a yellow Post-it note stuck to the door frame. "I will be over to see you this afternoon. Roland" it read. *Now I know his sudden appearance is no coincidence.*

She looked into the office and saw that Jean was not there. Just as she was turning away, Jean returned, greeted Adrienne and saw the note which she removed.

"Do you have a few minutes, Jean?" Adrienne asked. "I have something I need to talk with you about."

Adrienne explained the situation and asked for her advice. Jean was well acquainted with Kate and Serena who had been at the museum much longer than she had. She remembered being very impressed with Susan when she had interviewed her. In addition, from comments made by other staff members, she knew they were all well respected at Summerston.

"I will look into it and get back to you," she told Adrienne.

"Thank you," she responded and left the office.

As Adrienne reached the door into the museum's reception area, she heard Roland greeting Jean. It was as if he had been standing somewhere in the hall waiting for her to leave. Apparently, he did not intend to wait until the afternoon to talk with Jean.

Adrienne was extremely disturbed by Roland's obvious interference. James Grover was Jean's immediate superior and James reported to Thurston. The two of them had been with Roland at the festival. They would say whatever Roland wanted them to say. And Jean, not wishing to jeopardize her job, would have to do whatever she was told by James. This was extremely upsetting. Roland had stacked the deck. The question of how far he would go was not yet clear.

Adrienne returned to Richmond House where she found Serena, Kate and Susan sorting papers at the large table. She called to Elinor who came into the former dining room from her office. Adrienne recounted what had happened. The three volunteers were quite angry about Roland and vowed to contact their witnesses and get in writing what had really happened so that they could provide Jean with this information.

It never occurred to them that Jean would not ask to hear their side of the story. While they knew her as someone who carefully played by the rules, they also felt that she was a fair person. Serena and Kate remembered with fondness the most appropriate and clearly well thought out gifts she had purchased on behalf of the museum to commemorate their most recent service anniversaries.

THIRTY

Serena, Kate and Susan spent the next two weeks wrapping up the silent auction - getting the birdhouses delivered to those not present at the end of the festival, writing the artists, and organizing the project file. In addition, they helped Adrienne and Elinor finish the remaining thank you letters and put together the large festival notebook.

For her part, Elinor was still trying to get all of the invoices paid. She needed Roland's approval for anything over $500. He rarely responded to her requests in a timely fashion. This had been especially embarrassing the day before the festival. Martin Sonderly had come into the office to get his check, and she had to tell him that it was not ready. He set up the sound system every year and always received half of the payment after it was installed. The other half was paid when the festival was over. She had requested approval for both checks a month before the festival to insure that Finance would have time to prepare them.

While Roland deliberately delayed Martin's payment, he was very quick to approve the invoice from Dining Unlimited. Even before Adrienne had seen it. When it arrived, she checked every detail against the contract - as she did with each invoice submitted by a vendor or service provider. She quickly noticed that the festival was being charged twice what was specified in the contract.

Originally, Nicki had tried to charge $90 per person. The festival executive committee was aware that other bidders had estimated between $40-$45 and, as a result, had refused to accept her bid. Although Roland knew that he could force Adrienne to use Dining Unlimited, he also knew he could not force the committee to accept too high a bid since they had made it clear the festival budget had to be trimmed.

But now Nicki had charged $45 per person times 500 people when only 250 had actually accepted. That brought the price back to her original $90 per person. Adrienne immediately sent an email to Roland asking to have the bill reviewed. She received a response, not from Roland, but from a member of his department. Once again he was careful not to put anything in writing, not to take responsibility for something that might prove problematical. According to the email, Roland had reviewed the bill, and it was to be paid.

Adrienne contacted Finance and told them to pay the bill per Roland's instructions.

Several days later Adrienne went to Roland's office for her bi-weekly meeting. She was extremely nervous, almost sick to her stomach, after their last encounter.

As it turned out, it was an entirely different Roland who greeted her. He started off by complimenting her on the attractive navy trimmed hunter green jacket from Chico's that she wore. He especially noted how the fit and color suited her. Roland added that the gold medallion necklace, a gift from her mother, was the perfect accessory.

Finding this just a bit bizarre from someone who had been so abusive during their last meeting, she was glad when he finally moved on to business. He informed her that he had reviewed the bill from Dining Unlimited, and it should not be paid after all. Nicki needed to make some changes. He, of course, made it sound as if he had discovered the overcharges, not Adrienne.

She wondered if he had realized that the museum's chief financial officer might question such a large bill. He had attended the preview and would know Nicki could not justify the charge considering what had been served and the number of guests in the tent.

Roland agreed with her handling of several complaints about the parking, approved the agenda for the wrap-up meeting with the festival executive committee and confirmed the meeting date. While he had still neglected to compliment her on the festival, at least, he had been cooperative and pleasant. Had Adrienne not been so relieved by his disarming change in attitude, she would have been suspicious.

THIRTY-ONE

She returned to Richmond House and described the meeting to Elinor. It was only after she finished that she noticed the stricken look on Elinor's face.

"Has something happened," she asked. "You look very upset."

Without saying anything Elinor handed her an email that had arrived while Adrienne was out.

"Serena, Susan and I have all received letters from Jean Howard telling us that we must turn in our volunteer credentials because we may no longer work at Summerston. We have been accused of making inappropriate remarks to unnamed staff members," wrote Kate. "Susan called her and asked for details in writing. She informed Susan that would not be possible. Susan told Jean that we would be consulting an attorney before we turned in our credentials and asked if we had the option of resigning. Jean very quickly responded in the affirmative leading Susan to believe that dismissal had not been her idea."

Adrienne was so angry she could hardly speak. "No wonder Roland was so charming and agreeable this morning. He knew all about Jean getting rid of our volunteers."

"If I didn't need this job so much, I would quit."

"Which is exactly what he wants, of course," responded Elinor.

"And with more layoffs expected, perhaps, we will both be gone, anyway. He may just decide to get rid of us and not worry about what it will cost the museum."

"I wonder if he may already have decided that," said Elinor. "While you were gone, I had a very strange phone call from Edith in PR. You know how she likes to gossip, and she often seems to know things before they are made public."

The manager of public relations had to be notified in advance of major layoffs in order to prepare a press release. Such information should have been her purview alone. That was not always the case. Her employees had been known to use such information to warn friends that they were going to lose their jobs or to taunt others with little hints, causing them alarm.

"She asked a lot of questions about my husband, Ed. How many hours he worked in the library, did he like his work, did he want more hours, that kind of thing. I just thought she was being friendly, but after thinking about it I wondered if it was meant as a warning. If I am laid off, does he have enough hours to cover us." Elinor's husband worked part time cataloging special collections and arranging displays.

"We may get more than a hint of our futures at the festival executive committee wrap-up meeting with Dr. Kent and Roland in a week. When I stopped in finance to tell them to hold up on the Dining Unlimited bill, I ran into Carl. He told me on the quiet that Roland has asked for all kinds of figures for the past five years, comparing the festival and The Textile Market. Carl said he has a funny feeling that the figures Finance sends Roland will not, necessarily, be the figures shown to the committee. Or, at least, not in the original format."

Feeling as low spirited as Elinor, Adrienne went upstairs to her office to contact Serena, Kate and Susan.

THIRTY-TWO

Several days later, following a visit to Kate's attorney's office, the three now former volunteers met at Serena's home and discussed their options.

"I feel like dejá vu," said Susan. "You remember what happened to my father-in-law last year?"

"That was almost criminal. I still don't believe some of the Board members did not help him," said Serena.

James Penn was a retired engineer who had always loved boating. Upon retirement he had joined a number of his friends who volunteered at the Five Points Marine Museum. Specializing in the construction of ship models, he and four other men had met twice a week to create a number of extraordinary ships. Wishing to display them properly, they had sought a donor for the materials needed to construct some very special cases. Each one would not only enable visitors to walk around the enclosed model but could be raised or lowered depending upon the height of those studying them. This would be most advantageous for the many school tours offered at the museum. James had solicited a friend and been delighted with his generosity.

Taking the donation to the museum director, James made it clear that this was a designated donation to be used only for the display cases. The director had taken the check and agreed.

Three months passed before the men were able to locate a supplier for what they wanted. The materials were ordered and delivered to the museum. However, the director refused to pay the bill which accompanied the delivery. James received a call from the supplier and was shocked to learn that the director claimed no responsibility, saying the museum had not placed the order and would not honor the invoice.

He immediately contacted the director who told James there had been an emergency with the heating system in the boat house, and the donation had been used for that purpose. When reminded that the money had been designated by the donor for the display cases, the director claimed that nothing was in writing. James was furious and wrote a letter to the chairman of the museum board. Like his daughter-in-law was to learn, exposing such practices is not always appreciated. The chairman sided with the director who then informed James that while they were grateful for his past efforts, he was no longer welcome at the museum as a volunteer. James had called the donor and explained what happened. A very kind man who preferred not to become embroiled with unpleasant situations, he had expressed concern for James, but said he did not wish to pursue the matter.

And now Susan was faced with the same type of dilemma. How ironic. But she was determined to do something about this one.

THIRTY-THREE

The lawyer's appraisal of the situation was discouraging. Susan, Kate and Serena could sue for defamation of character. It would not be easy to prove because Roland had so carefully avoided putting anything in writing. It would be his word against Adrienne's, and he could maintain that the dismissal was the action of an overzealous manager of volunteers. To counter that a number of employees would have to be called to give depositions. Having experienced Roland's vindictiveness first hand, the three had no doubt he would see to it that those employees testifying against him would lose their jobs.

They considered and rejected a number of ideas. The Board needed to understand what a detriment Roland was to Summerston. And he needed to understand that he had picked on the wrong people.

All of a sudden, Kate smiled and asked, "What about contacting my friend, Trevor Erskine, who sponsored the birdhouse auction?"

"He also planned to write to Dr. Kent about the poor publicity, but after reading the response we received, he decided a letter from him would serve no purpose," remembered Serena.

"As a donor to the craft festival, someone with his name in the program, you would think they should pay attention to his concerns," argued Susan.

"They certainly should listen to him. But, remember, Roland has completely ignored him. He did not ask anyone to contact Trevor to thank him for his donation or to encourage future support," Kate reminded Serena and Susan.

"That was certainly an oversight, wasn't it?" Serena said with the first real sense of optimism she had felt all day.

The three ladies looked at each other and smiled.

"I think he is the perfect person to instigate Roland's fall from grace. Let me handle this - I'll keep you posted." Kate, also, was feeling more encouraged and rather amused by their decision.

THIRTY-FOUR

The following week Roland strolled into Thurston's office and made himself comfortable in one of the chairs in front of the large mahogany desk. He and Thurston had made sure to find the best pieces of furniture for their offices when they came to work at the museum. No institutional metal or battered furniture for them.

With a smug look on his face, he announced, "I have won half of the daily double and will complete the victory this afternoon."

Thurston looked up from the catalog he was reading. "Do tell."

"Adrienne no longer has her meddling, precious volunteers. I have seen to that. And by four-thirty the craft festival will be history."

"Oh, you have been a busy boy," joked Thurston. "To what do you owe your extraordinary success?"

They both laughed, and Roland outlined his campaign to demoralize Adrienne by having her volunteers dismissed. Then he explained the final action which would rid him of the annoying festival. Thurston was impressed, and they both went off to have a congratulatory lunch.

At 3:30 that afternoon, the wrap-up meeting for the festival executive committee was called to order by its chairman, Jeffrey Longhurst. A member of the museum's board, he was an avid collector of folk art, and his family had been supporters of the museum since its inception. In addition to the eight committee members, Adrienne, Roland and Dr. Kent were also in attendance. As usual, Elinor was present to take the minutes and to tape record the meeting.

Jeffrey moved through the agenda very efficiently with a lively discussion on several issues. At the conclusion of the meeting, Dr. Kent surprised everyone by announcing that he wished to hold a private session with committee members. Adrienne and Elinor were excused and replaced by the museum's chief financial officer, Donald Lewis.

Roland passed out copies of the financial report that Carl in Finance had warned Adrienne about the week before.

Without any preliminary comments, Dr. Kent bluntly declared, "At the next board meeting I plan to announce that the museum will no longer hold a craft festival."

Oblivious to the astonished expressions greeting this, he continued, "From the financial figures it is clear that the festival has run its course. It is losing popularity and costing the museum too much money in staff time. Before it starts actually losing money, it should be discontinued. On the other hand, you can see that The Textile Market is profitable and a more viable source of income for the future. If you have any questions about this report, I am sure Donald can answer them."

Jeffrey was absolutely flabbergasted at the arrogance of Dr. Kent. How could he possibly think he had the right to override a board-appointed committee and make such a decision? From the looks being exchanged among the other committee members, it was obvious Jeffrey was not alone in his opinion.

When no one said anything, Dr. Kent began to realize that his approach may have been a bit too abrupt. He began to backtrack. "Er, what I am saying, ah, suggesting is for the committee to go over these figures and decide what to do about the festival. I am sure that once you have looked at the evidence you will come to the same conclusion that I have reached."

Asking the committee to get back to him as soon as possible, he left the room followed by Roland and Donald.

Putting a finger to his lips to silence any discussion, Jeffrey quietly announced this was neither the time nor, especially, the place to talk about what had just occurred. He set a mutually agreed upon date for the committee to reconvene at his office downtown. Still shaking their heads, the committee members left the conference room and went down the stairs and out of the building, heading for their cars.

Roland watched them leave from his office window and smiled. *They never knew what hit them, and Jeffrey is no leader. He is far too busy to spend time on this, and the others act like they care, but when an effort is involved, they'll fold.*

THIRTY-FIVE

L ess than a week after the meeting, Dr. Kent telephoned Jeffrey Longhurst at his office.

"Good morning," he said, "I was wondering what you and the festival committee have decided."

Barely able to control his temper, Jeffrey replied, "I will let you know after the committee has had a chance to review the figures." *The nerve of him*, he muttered, returning to the letter he was composing on his computer.

Later that afternoon, he called Donald Lewis at the museum. In preparation for the committee meeting he wanted the full budgets for each fundraiser. There was no way to compare each event without seeing the details. The hand-out the committee had received was inadequate.

To Jeffrey's surprise Donald hesitated and finally said he would need to check with Dr. Kent and call him back. In the past, any time a board member asked for figures or reports, they were sent immediately.

When he arrived at the office the next morning, Jeffrey found a note on his desk from his assistant. Dr. Kent, himself, had called. It would take too much time to gather all of the budgets together. The information supplied to the committee was certainly sufficient to make a decision.

Jeffrey knew very well this was not true. The budgets were readily available in the computer files, and it would take only a few minutes to transmit them to him by email. He could then send them on to all the committee members. This was, definitely, suspicious.

Resorting to some deception of his own, Jeffrey was able to obtain copies of the budgets and had his assistant send them to the committee members.

Four days later the committee assembled in the conference room adjacent to Jeffrey's office. He started the meeting by describing the first call from Dr. Kent.

"He, obviously, thought he could rush this through. That we would just accept the meager information he supplied us," said one of the members who was a CPA.

Jeffrey then related his conversation with Donald Lewis and the message from Dr. Kent. Everyone agreed that something just did not add up. There was no reason a board-appointed committee should be denied financial figures.

"One of Dr. Kent's main concerns is the cost of museum staff time," observed a committee member who, like Jeffrey, was also on the museum's board. "He cited this as one of the primary reasons the festival should be discontinued. The figures he gave us show a large expense for museum personnel for the craft festival but almost nothing for the market. We know Adrienne spends almost the same amount of time on both fundraisers. Other museum staff members perform similar jobs for each event - publicity, mailings, sponsor solicitations. I cannot believe these numbers are correct. And that raises questions about all of the other expense comparisons."

His skepticism was shared by the others sitting around the table.

"And what about the way Roland keeps saying he could raise the same amount as the festival with just a few phone calls?" asked another committee member. "Since there is no limit to the amount of money that needs to be raised for the museum, why doesn't he make those calls!"

The committee spent the next hour carefully reviewing the figures and comparing them to the budgets Jeffrey had obtained. There was no question that the figures provided to the committee had been carefully manipulated to support Dr. Kent's proposal.

After discussing the many ways in which the festival benefited the museum and the need for its continuance, the committee developed several ideas to improve it as well as a plan for dealing with Dr. Kent and Roland. Most of the members had never taken to Roland and did not trust him. Now they no longer trusted Dr. Kent. Not only had the two of them presented tainted financial figures, but one committee member was able to provide several examples of their involvement with outright sabotage to the recent festival.

The next morning Jeffrey called Dr. Kent and set up a meeting. Because he had to be out of the country on business for several weeks, Jeffrey set a date on a Friday that was three weeks away. Dr. Kent was not at all pleased with this, but there was nothing he could do.

"I will be sure to have the appropriate staff members there," he informed Jeffrey.

"No," came the reply. "The only other staff member with whom I wish to meet is the chief financial officer."

Before calling Dr. Kent, Jeffrey had made another call

to arrange for someone to accompany him to the meeting. A very active supporter of Summerston, this donor was a force in the community and, if necessary, could rally tremendous support to retain the festival. Judith Jordan was someone who would, without hesitation, stand up to Dr. Kent and eloquently let him know how important the event was to the museum.

Little did Jeffrey know that she would be prepared to do far more than that.

THIRTY-SIX

J udith Jordan sat at her desk staring out the window in front of her. She hardly saw the gently flowing river or the blue heron in his usual spot, among the wild flowers, watching for fish. While Jeffrey's call had been disquieting, she had something even more serious on her mind. In front of her was a legal pad with five names on it and the same entry next to each. She had just finished calling professors at five area colleges and received identical, disturbing responses to her questions.

In memory of her late husband, Judith had funded a number of different educational programs over the years to promote interest in folk art. Her husband was an avid collector and enjoyed introducing others to the genre. She had carefully researched the programs at local colleges close to the museum and had found fertile ground for a cooperative effort with Summerston.

Working with the professors of textile arts at five schools, she had prepared a proposal for the museum. Summerston's education division manager was delighted and invited a staff member, Tory Edmunds, to join in the discussions with Judith. She and Judith were both impressed by Tory's creativity and organizational skills. Judith was very pleased when Tory was put in charge of the program. Tory and the educators met and developed a 12 week course using the facilities and staff at Summerston. Offering such a course starting in January fit perfectly with the colleges' schedules and with Summerston - these were always the three slowest months for the museum.

Judith was puzzled when no one contacted her to report on the program but decided everyone at the museum was probably busy with the lectures and workshops offered at the craft festival and with final exams at the colleges. As the end of May approached, however, she became very concerned and called Summerston.

Asking the operator to connect her to Tory Edmunds, she was surprised to learn that no one by that name was listed as an employee. Now she was not only concerned but completely baffled. When the operator asked if there was someone else to whom she would like to speak, Judith asked for the manager of the education division. Her phone was answered by a recording explaining she was out of the office for the next six days.

Not wanting to wait any longer, Judith began contacting the five colleges. Several of the professors were reluctant to speak with her - some sounding openly hostile. She soon discovered why. They had been contacted by the museum and told that the donor had not been forthcoming with the funding after all - probably the economy - and that Tory had been laid off. Needless to say, they were very angry and were forced to make other arrangements for their students. No easy task.

When her son, Stewart, came into her study, she explained what she had discovered.

"What do you think happened to the money?" was his first question and the one uppermost in her mind.

"That is exactly what we are going to find out," she replied and explained what she wanted him to do.

Stewart called Donald Lewis and introduced himself.

"My mother is working with her financial advisor on another donation to Summerston. She has forgotten if her last one was designated for a specific purpose or undesignated - you know how that can be as one gets older," he lied. He didn't know anyone with a sharper mind than his mother.

Donald was sympathetic, his own mother was exhibiting signs of dementia. He looked up Judith's file in the computer's donor data base and told Stewart, "The last check - for $25,000 - was received on September 10 and did have a designation for the Ethan Jordan Educational Fund. However, there is a notation showing that it was changed to Special Exhibitions Fund on October 19."

"Does it say who made that change?" asked Stewart.

Donald was pleased to see that the staffer making the notation had followed procedures and included the initials of the person making the request. He was very proud of the way his staff paid careful attention to details. In this case, he had no idea how very important that would prove.

So that there would be no chance to compare notes, Judith had called Roland at the very same time that Stewart was calling the museum's chief financial officer.

"Roland, this is Judith Jordan. I wonder if you could be so kind as to help me with a little puzzle," she asked in a somewhat befuddled tone.

"Of course, what can I do for you," he responded.

"Last fall I made a donation for a cooperative program between Summerston and five local colleges. I was wondering if you could tell me what happened with that program."

Caught off guard, Roland was silent for a few moments. "I do remember that. It was actually handled by the education division. If you don't mind, I will contact them and get the information for you. Will I be able to reach you later this afternoon?"

"Oh, of course, Roland. Any time. I so appreciate your help," she almost simpered.

Having completed his call, Stewart heard the last part of her conversation and could hardly control his laughter until she hung up. She joined him for a moment, "He is such an …" However, her amusement vanished when Stewart told her what the CFO had revealed.

THIRTY-SEVEN

For his part, Roland was not laughing. He had known that this day might come. However he was well rehearsed. He just needed to make it look as if he was researching her question. His answer had been carefully prepared ever since he and Dr. Kent had used the donation for something else.

Last October one of the major donors for the weathervane exhibition had suddenly dropped out twenty-four hours before the deposit was due, leaving a shortfall of $35,000. If Summerston could not make the payment, the traveling exhibition would not come to the museum. The final payment, due in March, would be covered by another donation, but that donation would not be available until then. And it was unlikely that Roland could raise the money and have it transferred in the limited time available.

In a panic, Roland began looking at places from which he might "borrow" the necessary funds. He remembered that in early September he had signed a $25,000 agreement with Mrs. Jordan for an education program. Having met her and her son, he decided they would not notice if the program did not proceed.

With few, if any, other options he went to discuss the situation with Dr. Kent.

"We must come up with the money. Several board members strongly recommended this exhibition, and we are the only museum on the East Coast that will have it," Dr. Kent told Roland.

"I think I can transfer $25,000 from a designated account," offered Roland. "You have met Judith and Stewart Jordan. She seems rather vague. Her son always does the talking, and she just smiles a rather vacant smile. However, while he is pleasant and outgoing, he strikes me as a bit of an air head. She is funding a school program that is being organized by our education division. I can simply explain to them that Mrs. Jordan changed her mind, and the money won't be available this year after all. I guarantee you, the Jordans will not notice. Once the check was written, they forgot all about it."

"What will you tell Finance about changing the designation?" Dr. Kent asked.

"I'll explain that the schools cannot fit the program into their curriculum this year. Mrs. Jordan does not want the money going unused, so she has very graciously let us use the money for the upcoming exhibition."

"You don't think someone will check with her, do you?"

"No. They would never contact a high level donor without first consulting me," Roland assured him.

"Make it very clear that she wants to remain anonymous," Dr. Kent admonished him. "We don't want her name to appear as a sponsor. I do think she and her son might just notice that."

Roland laughed. "I suppose even they would."

Dr. Kent then brought up the issue of needing another $10,000 to cover the shortfall.

"We can take that out of The Textile Market account. By now there are enough deposits from vendors, donations from sponsors and money from advertisers," he said.

"That should cover everything," Dr. Kent observed.

"Well, there is one last loose end Some of the curators knew that Mr. & Mrs. Chambers were making the original $35,000 donation. How do we handle them?" asked Roland.

Dr. Kent thought for a moment and then suggested, "I will explain at the next meeting of department heads that they were unable to contribute as planned, but an anonymous donor stepped in and provided the necessary funding."

Satisfied that they had solved their problem, Roland left the director's office to make the necessary calls to insure the deposit check would be ready for delivery.

He also called Thurston.

"I have just learned that Mrs. Jordan is not going to fund that cooperative program with the five colleges after all."

"Oh, my," said Thurston. "I believe that donation provides most of the salary for one of the education division part-time staff members."

"You know how tight things are right now. There just isn't any extra money anywhere to cover that program," Roland told him.

Regretfully, because he was looking forward to the good publicity from this program, Thurston called the education division manager and passed on the bad news. That afternoon Tory Edmunds lost her job.

Of course, Roland and Dr. Kent did not know of the arrangements Judith Jordan had made with the professors and Tory for a report at the end of the program. Such information from the students, colleges and Summerston was designed to help her determine whether or not to fund cooperative efforts in the future. Because of this ignorance, Roland had no idea how damaging these lies would be eight months later.

THIRTY-EIGHT

Having waited the appropriate amount of time, Roland called Judith to report on his promised discussion with the education division.

"Mrs. Jordan, I am sorry if it took longer than expected," he apologized.

"Not a problem, Roland, it is so very kind of you to do this for me," she said avoiding a glance at Stewart who was listening to the speaker phone transmission.

"The current manager of the education division checked the records and was quite horrified to discover that the employee in charge of the program completely dropped the ball. She never set it up. The former manager retired suddenly due to illness and did not have a chance to brief her successor on everything. This particular program slipped through the cracks."

"Oh, my Roland, this is terrible. What must the schools think?" she asked.

"The manager will be in touch with everyone and assure them that the program will be held next year. I cannot tell you how dreadfully sorry I am. I will, of course, inform Dr. Kent. I know he will be in touch with you. We sincerely hope that you will let us keep your donation to use next year," he said trying to sound very abject.

"Well …" she paused just long enough to make Roland uneasy. "I do want the course to be available to those wonderful students who work so hard."

"I know how grateful they will be," Roland quickly asserted.

Judith considered keeping him hanging for a few days, but she had too much on her mind and wanted to get the little toad off the phone and not have to speak with him again.

"Please tell the education manager to go ahead with the course for next year," she finally told him. "And it really won't be necessary to have Dr. Kent call me."

"We are so grateful, Mrs. Jordan. You are being very understanding, and I know I speak for our whole staff when I …" *yadda, yadda, yadda,* thought Judith as she tuned him out. When he finally stopped, she reiterated that it was not necessary for Dr. Kent to call and bid him good- bye.

"Now what?" asked Stewart.

"In about three weeks, Jeffrey Longhurst is meeting with Dr. Kent to discuss the craft festival and wants me to go with him. I think we should both attend. And we will be discussing much more than Dr. Kent's desire to cancel the festival."

THIRTY-NINE

The next day, Roland was feeling quite proud of himself. He had successfully placated Mrs. Jordon, one
of the museum's more important donors, and he
needn't worry about her anymore. Of course, he now had
to replace the $25,000, but he thought he could handle
that without too much effort. Earmarking funds from
the recent craft festival for a special educational program
would be easy enough. And he would think up something
to tell Thurston when he informed him that money was
now available for the cooperative program. But there was
no hurry.

He logged on to his email and fumed. *Why are all of
these Fireboard Seminar reservations still being sent to me.
They are supposed to go to Jody. I told her that last month.*
Without opening any of the offending emails, he forwarded them to the museum intern responsible for the August
seminar and deleted them from his incoming mail.

He picked up the phone and left a message on her
voicemail firmly informing her that he did not want to see
any more of those reservation emails.

Ten minutes later his phone rang. Assuming it was
Jody returning his call, he did not bother to check the
caller ID.

"Mr. Veasel? Security. Someone just noticed one of the tires on your car is flat. Think you need to take a look and…"

Roland hung up before the caller could finish, put on his sport coat and raced out of the office. He had an important meeting downtown in two hours and could not be late.

As he was leaving the building, a tall, dark-haired man carrying several file folders and wearing a non-descript navy raincoat entered just as the door was closing behind Roland. The man quickly climbed the stairs and, making sure he was unobserved, entered Roland's office. Putting on a pair of surgical gloves, he closed the door, took a letter out of one folder and tucked it in the middle of the large pile of papers filling the in basket on Roland's desk top.

Taking a cell phone out of his pocket, he punched a single number.

"Wait until I adjust the date," he said when someone answered.

Carefully noting which screen was on the computer, he exited it and changed the date on the computer.

Fortunately, once the system was running no password was necessary, so it was a simple matter to open Roland's email.

"Send the message."

An email which included "Fireboard Seminar Reservation" in the subject line appeared.

Clicking "reply" he sent a response.

He then reset the computer date and spoke into the phone, "Have those other messages sent."

After putting the cell phone in his pocket, he watched with satisfaction as a number of emails from different addresses but each with "Fireboard Seminar Reservation" in the subject line appeared below the first one.

He returned the computer to its original screen, carefully opened the door and removed his gloves. Placing them in his coat pocket, he checked to be sure no one was nearby. Had he encountered anyone, he would have just been an employee delivering files. If asked about him later, no one would remember anything special or that he was not wearing a security badge.

As he was walking back to the visitor center, Roland was on his cell phone in the staff parking lot calling Security to change his tire. He would not return to his office for some time. Before he did, numerous emails concerning museum business requiring his attention would arrive insuring he would pay no attention to the "reservation" emails before forwarding them to Jody. And leaving her another angry voicemail message.

FORTY

"**G**ood morning, Adam Payne's office. May I assist you?" came the polite response to his phone call.

"Yes, my name is Trevor Erskine. I would like to invite Mr. Payne to join me for lunch to discuss an exhibition sponsorship at the Summerston Museum."

"One moment, please."

"Adam Payne here, I understand you have an interest in the Summerston, Mr. Erskine."

"Yes, indeed, I do. I was a sponsor, on a rather small scale, for the recent craft festival. Testing the waters, if you will. Now I would like to explore a more substantial involvement. I apologize for the short notice, but I have just had a luncheon date with Dr. Kent and Roland Veasel confirmed. I hope that you can join us at noon next Friday at La Tasse d'Or," Trevor explained, naming one of the finest restaurants in the city.

While Trevor really did not care whether Adam Payne, Chairman of the Summerston Board of Trustees, came or not, he did want to be sure that he was aware of the scheduled luncheon meeting.

"Let me check my calendar." After a few moments of silence, Adam's strong baritone voice returned to the line.

"Yes, that would be fine. I look forward to meeting you."

Trevor returned the sentiment and, smiling to himself, hung up the phone.

Several minutes later he dialed the number of the restaurant and added one more to the reservation.

FORTY-ONE

A week later, Trevor stood in front of the imposing facade of La Tasse d'Or with its striking gold and black trim. Admiring the leaded glass door insets, he entered and approached the maître d'. Told that he was the first of his party to arrive, he left his coat in the cloakroom and took a seat on one of the comfortable leather benches set into the walls. His wait was a short one. Close behind a large party of smartly dressed women, a single man in a well tailored grey suit and navy striped tie entered the foyer. Recognizing him from his photos in the Summerston magazine, Trevor rose and introduced himself to Adam Payne.

They decided to be seated to await Dr. Kent and Roland. Adam was impressed with the gentleman facing him across the elegantly set round table. He was handsome in a rugged sort of way with a full head of dark chestnut brown hair and hazel eyes. Although dressed in a sport coat and coordinating slacks, he still exuded an air of formality. Even his somewhat whimsical tie, sporting tiny bears, did not detract from his sophisticated fashion statement.

They made small talk for a few moments and then discussed Summerston with Trevor exhibiting a comprehensive knowledge of and interest in the museum. He

135

explained that he resided in California but did a great deal of traveling as the managing director of his late mother's foundation. She had been a devoted patron of the arts on the west coast, and upon her death a private, family foundation had been established to continue that support. Annually, he and his sisters distributed a considerable amount of money to institutions all over the country, usually on an anonymous basis.

A friend from the area who had known Trevor's mother and her interest in folk art had told Trevor about Summerston's craft festival. Looking for information about the festival and the museum, he checked its website. The festival section about the painted birdhouse auction intrigued him. Making a small donation, he permitted his name to be listed in the program in order to gauge the response of Summerston to its sponsors. He frankly admitted to the board chairman that he had been disappointed when no one from the museum, except Adrienne, showed any interest in his support. This, he felt, was an oversight, especially in these tight economic times.

"Even small donors should be encouraged because you never know what they might do in the future." He hastened to add, "The craft festival staff was extremely attentive and appreciative."

In spite of this omission, he had decided to pursue the sponsorship of an exhibition at Summerston because he was most impressed with its collection, its restoration and conservation programs and its research facilities. It was an institution of which his mother would have approved.

Adam expressed his concern that Trevor had not been contacted and suggested they discuss this with Dr. Kent and Roland. Glancing at his watch, he was suddenly aware that half an hour had elapsed, and they had not arrived.

"Let me find out if they have been held up," he said pushing back his chair and leaving the table.

Trevor suppressed a smile and picked up his menu.

The maître d' showed Adam to one of the restaurant's private telephone booths. Closing the door and seating himself in a dark green leather chair he took out his address book and laid it on the small mahogany desk. Looking at the numbers for Summerston, he decided to call Dr. Kent first. No one answered, and the system switched to Dr. Kent's voicemail. Not wanting to leave a message, he tried Roland's office. Again, voicemail responded. Finally, he called Dr. Kent's secretary.

To his relief Elizabeth Markham answered. Identifying himself, he explained that he was waiting for Dr. Kent and wondered if he had been delayed in leaving the museum.

"I know he left about forty-five minutes ago, Mr. Payne, but I don't believe he was going into the city. I am pretty sure he said his wife was picking him up, and they were headed to a birthday party for a relative in Cloverton," she responded. "But let me look at his calendar."

While he waited for her return, he thought about what Elizabeth had just told him. Cloverton was a good hour south of the museum - the opposite direction from the city. And you did not suddenly get invited to a birthday party. This had to have been planned for some time.

"I was correct," Elizabeth said a little breathlessly. "It is marked on his calendar that he will be out the rest of the afternoon. Would you like me to call him on his cell phone for you?"

"No, I certainly do not want to disturb a family party. I could not reach Roland, either. He was also supposed to meet with Mr. Erskine and me for lunch. Is there any way to find out if he was intending to come?" asked Adam.

"I know I saw him go out around noon, but let me check with his staff."

Elizabeth left her office and went down the hall looking in offices. Finally, she found Edwina eating a sandwich at her desk while she checked a list of names.

"Adam Payne is on the phone and says Roland was supposed to meet him for lunch today at noon, but I saw Roland leaving the building just about that time. Do you happen to know if he was going to La Tasse D'Or?"

"Oh, some people have all the luck. I wouldn't mind being invited to have lunch at La Tasse D'Or. But I'm pretty sure that wasn't where Roland was going. Earlier today he told me he and Thurston were heading to Charley's for lunch and then to take a look at an exhibition at one of the nearby galleries. He was very vague about when he was returning. I specifically remember because he is supposed to review a donor list with me this afternoon." Clearly, Edwina was annoyed.

Back at her own desk, Elizabeth reconnected with Adam Payne and explained that she was very sorry, but it seemed Mr. Veasel had gone to lunch with another staff member. No fan of Roland, she was tempted to elaborate but resisted the temptation in the name of professionalism.

Extremely disconcerted, Adam returned to the table. Perhaps, Trevor had mistaken the date. He could not believe that both Dr. Kent and Roland had managed to forget such an important luncheon.

"Is something wrong?" Trevor innocently asked, seeing the rather perplexed expression on Adam's face.

"I am a little confused," confessed Adam. "I don't want to insult you, but is there any possibility of a misunderstanding as to the date you were to meet with Dr. Kent and Mr. Veasel? Neither one of them is at the museum, and they have both gone to lunch elsewhere."

Trevor opened the zippered leather folder he had placed under his chair when they sat down earlier. Extracting copies of a letter and two emails, he scanned them quickly before passing them to Adam.

From what Adam read it was clear that Trevor had sent a letter to Roland asking for a meeting with him and Dr. Kent and suggesting a date which he would confirm by email. The email, sent a week ago, confirmed the date, time and location. A copy of Roland's response by email acknowledged that he and Dr. Kent would be at La Tasse D'Or on today's date at noon. There was no mistake.

Clearly embarrassed for the museum, Adam apologized profusely to Trevor. He could not imagine what had happened, but he would certainly look into it on Monday. While he could discuss the museum and some of the upcoming exhibitions in general terms, unfortunately, it would be impossible without Roland present to conclude any kind of a specific agreement regarding a sponsorship.

Trevor was most understanding but made it clear that his sisters would not be impressed with what had transpired. He was not sure he could convince them to support an exhibition at a museum whose Director and Associate Director of Philanthropy would both forget this kind of meeting. He would, of course, do his best. If he succeeded, he would be in touch with Roland at a later date.

He had invited everyone to the restaurant as his guests, but Trevor graciously accepted Adam's offer to treat him. While discussing a number of topics of mutual interest, they enjoyed a delicious four course lunch, impeccably served.

On the way out of the restaurant Adam collected his red and black plaid umbrella and Trevor his navy raincoat from the cloak room. Shaking hands they parted on amicable terms with Adam walking in the rain back to his office and Trevor handing the valet his car park check.

Trevor had spent a most pleasant afternoon with Adam and felt a slight twinge of guilt for what had just happened. But as the chairman of Summerston's board, Adam should be more knowledgeable about what was going on at the museum under the leadership of Dr. Kent. He was sure Adam would, eventually, agree that the education he had just received was well worth the cost of a lunch at La Tasse d'Or.

FORTY-TWO

The more Adam Payne thought about what had happened, the more concerned he became. Trevor Erskine was a man representing what appeared to be a very lucrative foundation, someone the museum should certainly be courting. It was Roland's responsibility to insure that all such donors were treated as sources of future income for the museum. Roland or someone in his department should have contacted him. To make matters worse, now both Roland and Dr. Kent had insulted Trevor by failing to meet him for lunch.

Having decided he needed to talk with Dr. Kent in person as soon as possible, he called Summerston Monday morning and made an appointment with Dr. Kent for 3:15 that afternoon. He also asked that Roland be present.

Adam arrived at Williams House a little after three and was greeted by Elizabeth Markham who took him into Dr. Kent's office. Adam was surprised to find him alone, but Dr. Kent explained that Roland was meeting with a donor and would be along in a few minutes.

Not wanting to wait, Adam approached the reason for his visit. "I was wondering why you and Roland did not meet Trevor Erskine and me for lunch on Friday?" he asked.

"Friday?" Dr. Kent looked surprised. "This past Friday?"

"Yes," responded Adam.

Flipping the pages of his desk calendar, he checked several Fridays and then looked up at Adam. "I don't see a luncheon engagement with you any Friday this month. Last Friday, I was at a family birthday party. And who did you say you were with?"

"Trevor Erskine."

"I must confess that name does not mean anything to me. Who is he?" queried Dr. Kent.

"He was a sponsor for the craft festival and was interested in sponsoring a future museum exhibition," explained Adam as he extracted three pieces of paper from his brief case.

Feeling rather defensive, Dr. Kent stared at Adam, "I really do not know what you are talking about. I am sure I would have remembered if you called me for lunch."

"Actually, Mr. Erskine contacted Roland by mail and then exchanged emails with him setting up the appointment," he explained as he handed Dr. Kent copies of the correspondence.

Looking at the copies, Dr. Kent had no doubt that a luncheon had been scheduled. A luncheon he was expected to attend.

At that moment Roland entered the room, offering his hand and apologies to Adam for keeping him waiting. He then proceeded to explain in some detail the importance of the donor he was with, completely oblivious to the uneasy atmosphere in the room. And to Dr. Kent's growing anger. *How could you put me in this position?*

"Roland, Adam has just been asking me why we were

not at a luncheon meeting with a Trevor Erskine on Friday," Dr. Kent said staring at him.

"With whom?" asked Roland.

"Trevor Erskine. He was a craft festival sponsor and wanted to talk with us about sponsoring a future museum exhibition," replied Dr. Kent.

"A sponsor of the birdhouse auction," added Adam.

"Oh, him," said Roland in disgust. "Adrienne made him up."

"What?" both Dr. Kent and Adam said at the same time.

"He doesn't exist. She wanted the program to look good; so she made up a fancy name - I think she added a title or a III or IV to his name. She wanted people to think she had sponsors when she didn't."

Clearly confused by this, Dr. Kent passed Roland the pages he had just examined.

Roland read them over and became furious. *She will pay for this.* Barely able to keep control of his temper he said, "I have never seen any of these before. Someone has made all of this up. I tell you he does not exist. He is a figment of Adrienne Monkton's imagination as are these," he tossed the pages onto Dr. Kent's desk.

"How can this be a fake when it obviously came from your computer?" asked Adam picking up the page bearing the reply from Roland.

"I can't understand why you don't believe me," Roland angrily replied. "I would not have missed something like that. Adrienne made him up, just ask her."

"And I can assure you that he is very real," said Adam. "I spent several hours with the man on Friday, and he most definitely exists."

Roland could hardly believe his ears. "You met him?" he asked, completely stunned.

"I did, indeed," responded Adam, by now exasperated with Roland's behavior.

"And just so that we can clear this up once and for all, I think we should take a look at your email for the dates in question," said Dr. Kent.

Roland felt absolutely betrayed. *How could Dr. Kent turn on him like this.*

Reluctantly, Roland led the way to his office and sat down at his desk. The others stood behind him looking at the computer screen. Using the paper copies as a guide, he nervously displayed his incoming emails and checked the first date. Nothing there from Trevor Erskine. He controlled a sigh of relief.

Of course, since that email had come in with "Fireboard Seminar Reservation" in the subject line, Roland had immediately forwarded it to Jody and then deleted it from his computer. Jody was still on vacation, but upon her return Tuesday, she would discover that the email from Trevor also confirmed the Friday luncheon and send it back to Roland. But for the moment, the email was not in his list of incoming mail.

With more confidence he switched to his "sent" mail and checked the date. There were only five emails on the date in question - not surprising since Roland hesitated to put most things in writing. Four contained recognizable museum email addresses. Having opened the fifth one, he stared at it in horror. There it was in black and white, his response to Trevor confirming the luncheon. *Impossible* he almost screamed out loud. *There is no way I sent that email. No way!*

144

Adam looked at Dr. Kent who addressed the back of Roland's head. "It would appear that you did correspond with Mr. Erskine after all, Roland. I cannot imagine why you did not tell me about the luncheon and why you now claim to know nothing about this correspondence."

Almost speechless, Roland turned around and stared at the two men. "I never sent that email. I don't know how I can make you understand that. Why would I send an email to someone I am convinced does not exist?"

Sadly shaking his head, Dr. Kent addressed Adam, "I feel very badly about all of this, and I will, personally, be in touch with Mr. Erskine. I am sure we can smooth things over with him."

"I will rely on you," Adam responded shaking hands with Dr. Kent and leaving Roland's office.

After he left, Dr. Kent looked at the still shaken Roland. "I don't know what happened here, but it had better not happen again."

Before Roland could respond, Dr. Kent went out the door and returned to his own office.

FORTY-THREE

R oland sat behind his desk, too astounded and confused to move. The ringing of the telephone startled him, and seeing it was Thurston he decided to answer it. He needed to commiserate with him about what had happened. However, Thurston was in a hurry and needed Roland to see if he still had a document they had been discussing on Friday. While searching through his in basket, he came across the letter from Trevor Erskine.

How could that be? Was it possible that he was under too much stress and really had missed the letter and the email?

His self doubts grew even more the next day when he received the email Trevor Erskine had, apparently, sent to him - the email he did not think existed. It was being returned by Jody with the comment: "I have taken care of his question about the seminar and I am returning this in case you did not retain a copy before forwarding it to me." *Why would I have forwarded this to her? I was only sending her Fireboard Seminar reservation emails. I would never have sent something about the luncheon to Jody.*

He looked more carefully at the subject line: "Fireboard Seminar Reservation and Luncheon". The first paragraph of the email contained a question about the seminar registration. The second paragraph confirmed the time and date for the luncheon. *I was automatically forwarding all of the Fireboard Seminar emails, but wouldn't I have noticed this one was different? Or did it just blend in with all the others?*

He decided to go for a walk and clear his head. Brushing past Edwina who had arrived at his office with a sponsorship contract, he headed down the stairs and out the door. Leaving the museum behind, he followed one of the paths that wound through the garden.

Either he was losing his mind or … wait a minute. Was it possible that someone was setting him up? Could someone have accessed his computer? You needed a security badge to enter Williams House. That means it must be someone on staff. Adrienne. No, he rejected her. She is not smart enough to think this up, and she wouldn't know when he was out of his office. It has to be someone who knew he was out of his office and knew that his computer would still be on. Of course, someone in IT could have hacked into his computer, but that didn't make any sense. He never bothered with them, and he couldn't see them doing it for someone else. And how did the letter get into his in basket unless someone was in his office to put it there. He thought of the various staff members who work in the building. Anyone of them could have gone to his office, and no one would have thought anything of it. But would any of them have taken the chance? If they'd been seen, even though it seemed normal, someone might have told him they were looking for him or had left something in his office. The whole museum is a pack of spies with employees reporting infractions on each other. Something that frequently worked to his advantage. But, seemingly, not this time.

He found a wooden bench, tucked under a tree in a

quiet part of the garden and sat down. Unaware of the beautiful surroundings, he continued to consider and then eliminate different staff members.

Could it be that Dr. Kent is trying to get rid of him? He certainly had not been supportive in the face of Adam's accusations. Of course, he had to put up a good front, but once Adam Payne had left, he was quite demeaning. He is well aware that I know things he has done - just look at the Jordan donation. I don't think he is about to fire me. But if he can make me look incompetent to the chairman of the board... No one will believe me in the future.

With those discouraging thoughts dominating his mind, he returned to his office and carefully checked all of the recent incoming and outgoing emails and his in basket to be sure there were no more potentially explosive documents waiting to be detonated.

FORTY-FOUR

After the fiasco with Adam Payne, Roland carefully avoided Dr. Kent. He knew that once the meeting with Jeffrey Longhurst was over and the craft festival was a thing of the past, he would be back in the director's good graces. Certainly he would be rewarded for all of his hard work. Without his calculated sabotage of the festival, harassment of Adrienne, and manipulation of the financial figures, the festival would have continued.

He was rather puzzled by his exclusion from today's meeting. According to Dr. Kent, Jeffrey had been most emphatic about only including Donald Lewis. It was understandable to want the CFO there, but as the department head responsible for the festival wasn't his presence necessary? *Did Jeffrey Longhurst really exclude him or had that actually been Dr. Kent's idea?* This new thought was most unwelcome and, unfortunately, fit all too well into the scenario he had developed while sitting in the garden.

Roland was actually supposed to be on vacation, taking a long weekend to visit the Pemberton Art Fair. He had planned his trip months ago. But now he couldn't stay away from the museum. Too much was a stake.

A little before ten, he made a point of going to the copier. From there he could see anyone coming up the stairs to Dr. Kent's office. Much to his surprise he saw Judith Jordan and her son, Stewart, ascend the staircase behind Jeffrey Longhurst.

What are they doing with him? They don't have any connection with the festival? Or do they? We certainly didn't think Jeffrey would bother to consult with other museum supporters. Apparently, he had. But if this is his first team, Jeffrey's going to strike out, he thought confidently and smiled to himself.

Looking to her right, Judith noticed Roland lingering by the copy machine. *I cannot imagine he even knows how to use that*, she thought uncharitably. Putting a sweet smile on her face and waggling her fingers at him, she called out in an almost sing song voice, "Oh, Roland, how nice to see you again."

Roland smiled and waved to her as if he had just noticed her standing on the landing. Before he could respond, Stewart took her arm and guided her down the hall. "Stop it," he hissed with a smirk. She just gave him one of her innocent looks.

Dr. Kent was coming out the door of his office to greet them as they reached the end of the hall. At first, he saw only Jeffrey and motioned to the conference room. "Donald is waiting for us. I thought we would be more comfortable in here."

As he turned to enter the adjacent door, he noticed Jeffrey was not alone. He was just as surprised as Roland to see the Jordans. He knew, of course, that they were generous donors to the museum but did not remember their having any association with the craft festival.

Replacing his puzzled frown with a welcoming smile, he shook hands with them and ushered everyone into the room. Donald Lewis rose to greet the newcomers. He was introduced to the Jordans and remembered seeing them at one of the exhibition previews. While Stewart appeared the same, Donald recalled him being with a lady who looked much older, wearing a nondescript, unfashionable dress. Mrs. Jordan now resembled a modern banker or corporation president in a perfectly tailored navy suit, white v-neck blouse, navy heels and subtle but obviously expensive gold jewelry. She carried a leather Coach brief-case.

After offering coffee, which no one accepted, Dr. Kent seated himself at the table and turned to Jeffrey, "I trust your committee has now studied everything and reached a conclusion."

Jeffrey pulled a pad, pen and several type-written sheets out of his briefcase. Putting on his reading glasses he consulted the papers. "Before we start, I would like to ask Stewart to record this meeting. We always tape the committee sessions, and I want to be sure there are no misunderstandings about what is said here."

Dr. Kent hesitated. He preferred that this particular meeting not be recorded. "Do you think that is really necessary? I'm sure we will all be able to remember what we discuss or be able to refer to our notes."

"No, I think it would be best. I am representing a board-appointed committee, and it is important to have a detailed record of the discussions to share with the other members," responded Jeffrey as Stewart placed a small tape recorder on the table.

At this point, Dr. Kent could hardly refuse. It would look as if he had something to hide.

Jeffrey turned to Donald and began to ask a series

of questions about the financial report that had been given to the committee at its June meeting. Dr. Kent was surprised that Jeffery had, obviously, spent a good deal of time studying the information. And that his questions were so detailed. They covered far more than the financial hand-out had revealed. He wondered where Jeffrey had obtained the information when he, himself, had refused to provide it.

It quickly became apparent that Jeffrey felt the figures on the hand-out had been manipulated to support Dr. Kent's desire to discontinue the festival. At several points in the discussion Jeffery remarked that the Summerston Craft Festival expenses appeared inflated while those of The Textile Market seemed unreasonably low. Donald's responses to these observations were unsatisfactory. In fact, he appeared rather uncomfortable discussing the figures Jeffrey was quoting from the report. It was almost as if he had not seen them.

Having exhausted his questions, Jeffrey turned to Judith and nodded.

Looking straight at Dr. Kent, Judith spoke in a strong, self-confident voice which he did not recognize but that matched her now more sophisticated appearance.

"In addition to being the museum's largest fundraiser, having an event like this provides an enormous public relations opportunity. Summerston's name is before the public for months. That arouses interest and leads people to the website. Add to that the wide appeal of the festival. People who would not normally come to the museum come for the festival and discover what Summerston is all about. In the future when you advertise an exhibition or an event, they remember that they had a good time;

so why not try it again. The craft festival demonstrates that Summerston is not a stuffy museum open only to curators and wealthy collectors. Without this kind of reputation the museum will not survive. I cannot stress strongly enough how important this particular event is to Summerston. Certainly, you must see this."

Aware that this was exactly what Dr. Kent did not want, anyone and everyone coming for a visit, Judith was curious to see how he would respond.

Thinking quickly, Dr. Kent put a spin on his actions that quite astonished Jeffrey, Judith and Stewart with its absurdity. "You know there have been some problems with the festival over the years. It did not seem as though anyone was taking them seriously. I figured this would get the committee's attention."

"The committee has always been responsive to your concerns, and the discussions at our last meeting clearly demonstrated that," replied Jeffrey. He was quite disgusted with Dr. Kent's response. Like the other committee members, he had lost all respect for him.

"It is clear that the committee can and will address any concerns you may have, Dr. Kent. That being the case, there should be no question of the festival continuing. Am I correct?" asked Judith

"Yes," responded Dr. Kent. *But I did not say in what form it will continue*, he thought to himself. In the unlikely event the committee did not agree with him, Dr. Kent and Roland had already discussed other ways to insure the festival's demise.

The men rose as if to leave, but Judith remained seated. "If you don't mind, Dr. Kent, my son and I have something we would like to discuss with you."

Jeffrey had been alerted that the Jordans had another issue to pursue, so he shook hands with Dr. Kent and bid goodbye to Judith and Stewart. Accompanied by Donald Lewis, he left the room.

Roland heard their voices in the hall and from his office window saw Jeffrey leave the building. *Where are the Jordans?* he wondered.

FORTY-FIVE

In the conference room, Stewart thanked Dr. Kent for taking the time to speak with them Although Stewart spoke courteously, Dr. Kent had the feeling he did not have a choice in the matter. He needed to completely reassess the way he dealt with the Jordans, something he found most aggravating.

"We would appreciate it if Roland Veasel could join us," Stewart said.

"I am afraid that he is on vacation today," Dr. Kent replied, now more curious than ever about the forthcoming discussion.

"Oh?" questioned Judith, "We spoke to him in the hall when we arrived."

"I did not realize he had decided to come in," said Dr. Kent who then left the room in search of Roland. On his way out he was met at the door by his secretary who informed him that Adam Payne was in her office waiting for the meeting with Jeffrey Longhurst to end. Apparently, the Jordans had asked him to participate in this unexpected discussion.

Dr. Kent stared at her in amazement. Now he was extremely concerned. After what had just occurred, Adam Payne's appearance was ominous, indeed. Getting control of his emotions, he asked her to bring Adam to the conference room and to find Roland and have him join them.

Roland assumed Dr. Kent had summoned him to report on the meeting and was somewhat alarmed to see the Jordans and the chairman of the board sitting at the table. Looking at Dr. Kent for assurance, he found none. Dr. Kent looked rather apprehensive. This did not bode well. Dr. Kent was always confident.

Seating himself next to Dr. Kent and across from the Jordans, he smiled at Judith. This time she did not return the smile. As Dr. Kent had realized earlier, he was suddenly aware that she had assumed an entirely different persona.

After an almost imperceptible nod from his mother, Stewart looked at Adam Payne sitting across from him and began, "In September of last year my mother donated $25,000 to Summerston for a cooperative venture involving five local colleges. Tory Edmunds from the museum's education division was to work with representatives from these colleges to develop the curriculum. The program was scheduled to begin in January of this year."

He looked at Adam to be sure he was following this. Satisfied that he was, Stewart continued, "My mother recently spoke with Mr. Veasel and discovered that the program was never established."

"That's correct," interrupted Roland. "As I explained to Mrs. Jordan earlier, the employee responsible failed to develop it. You said her name was Tory?" he asked looking at Stewart.

When Stewart indicated that was correct, he looked around the table and confidently concluded, "This Tory has been fired. The museum will, of course, work with the schools to schedule a program next year."

"Very interesting," observed Judith. "But not at all what the college representatives told me."

Roland and Dr. Kent both looked startled. Why would she have contacted anyone at the colleges?

As if responding to their unspoken question, she continued, "I had asked the students, professors and Tory to complete a questionnaire once the course was over so that I could decide whether to fund it again. When I did not hear anything, I tried to reach Tory. After learning that she was no longer at Summerston, I tried to reach her supervisor. When that was unsuccessful, I contacted the colleges. My reception was not a pleasant one."

Taking up the recitation Stewart elaborated, "They were very angry with her. The colleges had been working with Tory and promoting the program to their students. And then suddenly the museum's education division cancelled it, saying my mother changed her mind about the donation."

"After I spoke with the professors, I decided to call Roland," Judith added. "He said he did not know anything about the program, would look into it and call me back,"

"While my mother was talking with Roland, I called Donald Lewis," said Stewart. "He checked her records and reported that the designation for her donation had been changed on October 19 to Special Exhibitions Fund. A change she did not initiate."

"When Roland called back, you can imagine how appalled I was by his explanation which, as you have just heard, blamed Tory. Even if I hadn't known by then that the funds were re-directed, I would still have been suspicious of his excuse. I was extremely impressed with Tory. She did not seem like the kind of person who would drop the ball."

"And my mother is a very good judge of character," Stewart added looking directly at Dr. Kent and Roland.

For the first time Adam Payne spoke, "How could the fund designation be changed without your knowledge? Who would have that authority?" he asked, looking at Judith and Stewart.

"According to the records the request was made on behalf of my mother, and no questions were asked," responded Stewart.

"Is there any way to find out who made the request ?" asked Adam

Both Dr. Kent and Roland shifted uneasily in their chairs. Dr. Kent knew Roland had made the request and began figuring out how to distance himself from the repercussions. Of course, he had participated in the decision to transfer the funds, and he knew that Roland would not hesitate to involve him. Fortunately, by forgetting an important luncheon and claiming ignorance of it, Roland had just appeared to be incompetent in the eyes of the chairman. It seemed unlikely that Adam Payne would trust anything Roland had to say.

"According to Mr. Lewis, the staff member making the change noted in the file that the request came from D.K.," said Stewart, well aware of the bombshell he had just dropped. "That was, undoubtedly, the reason my mother was not contacted for confirmation."

Waiting for Roland to start explaining himself, Dr. Kent suddenly realized what had been said.

"That's impossible," he stammered. "I never made any

such request." As the words left his mouth, he realized how much he sounded like Roland trying to explain himself last Monday.

And he decided it would be best not to say anything else.

Unable to stop himself, Roland shouted, "No, but you told me to do it, figuring I'd take the fall. Had to protect your precious weathervane exhibition."

Stunned, everyone stared at the two men.

Into the silence Adam announced, "There is, obviously, a problem that needs to be addressed."

When setting up the meeting, Judith and Stewart had warned him there was a very strong probability that they had a case of financial malfeasance against Summerston which involved Dr. Kent and Roland. Adam had known the Jordans for many years and was sure they would not make such a claim unless they had absolute proof. His main concern was that no one's reputation be damaged unnecessarily, especially that of the museum. It was also important that no records be destroyed. Prior to the meeting he had taken the precaution of calling Henry Davis, Associate Director of Security, and asking him to come to the administrative offices.

"I think it would be best if you both take a leave of absence until we get this straightened out," he said looking at Dr. Kent and Roland. He went to the side table, picked up the conference room phone, dialed an extension and spoke too softly for those in the room to hear.

"Henry Davis will be here in a moment. Please give him your security badges. He will go with you, Roland, to your office so that you can get whatever personal effects you need. He will shut down the computer, and your password will become inactive. You may then leave the building. He will return here and go to your office with you, Daniel, and repeat the process. Any laptop computers must be left at the museum, at least for the time being. I am very sorry to do things this way, but given the seriousness of the allegations made by the Jordans and the evidence I have heard thus far, I don't have any choice. I will, of course, be in touch with the museum trustees later today."

Everyone looked up as the door opened and Henry Davis entered. Adam explained to him what was to happen and asked him to return to the conference room as soon as Roland had left the building.

Roland departed with Henry, and Adam once again went to the phone. He asked the museum operator to connect him with the head of IT. After introducing himself, Adam explained that there had been a problem with computers used by Dr. Kent and Roland. The computers were being shut down, and as soon as that was done he wanted the current passwords nullified. New ones would be created once the problem was solved. He knew this was a rather feeble excuse, and one that would lead to rumors, but he couldn't think of anything else on such short notice. Since a staff member could access his or her computer from off site, he did not want any tampering. He asked that he be notified on the conference room extension as soon as the passwords were invalidated.

Everyone then sat in silence until Henry returned and Dr. Kent left the room with him. Less than ten minutes later Henry re-entered the conference room. Adam introduced him to the Jordans and asked that he be seated. As Henry sat down opposite Judith, the phone rang, and Adam was told the passwords were no longer valid.

Thanking the head of IT he hung up and joined everyone at the table.

First, he made it clear to Henry that this was an extremely sensitive situation and that what was discussed in the conference room was strictly confidential. A retired police detective, Henry had been at the museum for ten years, was highly respected by the staff and known for his discretion.

Briefly, Adam outlined the allegation brought by the Jordans of financial malfeasance and the need to protect all records. He also had some concerns about possible involvement by Donald Lewis.

"I would like to speak with him now, and I may need you when I am finished. I would appreciate it if you waited in Elizabeth Markham's office," Adam explained to Henry.

Henry got up from the table, went out the door and down the hall. As he waited in the nearby office, he called the security officer on motor patrol. Without explanation he asked him to check on the staff parking area and let him know when Dr. Kent and Roland Veasel had left.

FORTY-SIX

Daniel Kent sat in his black BMW, his hands frozen on the steering wheel. *Damn Roland. How could I let him get me into this. I should never have listened to him.*

Needing someone to blame, Dr. Kent conveniently forgot his own arrogance that drove him to do whatever was necessary to succeed. At the hospital there had been suspicions that figures were not always what they seemed, but economic times were good, and nothing ever came to light.

Finally, turning the key, he backed out of his parking space and began driving away from Summerston. *Well, at least Jenny will be happy,* he thought, remembering how his wife had been wistfully talking about a four week trip to the Far East aboard the *Queen Victoria*. She was pleased when only six months after retiring from the hospital, he had taken on this new challenge. He was not someone who sat on a dock with a fishing pole or hit a golf ball four days a week. However, with the job came new and time-consuming responsibilities, the need for them to appear frequently at public functions and little time for vacations.

That any kind of scandal would be attached to his departure did not enter his mind. In his subconscious, he knew the board would do everything possible to avoid adverse publicity. And after all, they had hired him, announced his arrival with great fanfare and taken the credit for persuading him to become the museum's director. They were hardly going to admit they made a mistake. *No, they'll just say I decided to spend more time with my family. How many times have we heard that?* he thought ruefully. *Perhaps the public relations staff will think up something less trite. Not likely.*

Watching Dr. Kent's black car leave the parking lot, Roland, too, was justifying what had just transpired. Unable to control his shaking hands, he had been sitting in the car staring out at the brilliant blue sky and late flowering trees, but seeing nothing. *How could he have so misjudged the Jordans?* Roland prided himself on carefully evaluating people - learning their weaknesses, charming people into revealing themselves. *But it wasn't really my fault*, he decided. *The Jordans put on an act, they lied, they deceived everyone, they are the guilty ones.*

Having satisfied himself that he was the true victim, he began to calm down and was able to start the car. But, as he shifted into drive, another doubt assailed him. *Trevor Erskine. He cannot exist, he cannot exist.* He was shouting inside his head. *There is no way I could have misjudged that.* But the fact remained, Adam Payne said he met him, dined with him. And the board chairman was a serious, no nonsense man who did not go in for flights of fantasy. As much as it pained him to admit it, he just may have been wrong about Adrienne inventing him, wrong about the existence of Trevor Erskine.

Ten minutes later, the security guard patrolling the grounds reported to Henry Davis that both Dr. Kent and Roland Veasel had left Summerston.

FORTY-SEVEN

Alone with the Jordans, Adam apologized, "I cannot tell you how sorry I am that this happened. The education division will be instructed to contact the colleges immediately, and funds will be made available. If it is possible to re-hire Tory Edmunds to run the program, it will be done. For many years you have most generously supported Summerston. I hope we can earn your trust again."

Judith and Stewart appreciated Adam's obvious sincerity and expressed their gratitude for his prompt action regarding the cooperative program. They felt sure there was time to make it a reality next January.

Adam then conferred with them regarding the upcoming interview with Donald Lewis. "Before I discuss the misuse of your donation with the trustees, Judith, I want to verify the information we have. It is important to look at your donor file and have paper copies of it.

After Judith agreed that he should have the files checked, he continued, "Once we have done that, I need to discuss another issue with Donald."

Putting a file folder from his briefcase on the table, he opened it and took out several pages of handwritten notes and a financial report. "Jeffrey Longhurst told me about

Dr. Kent's refusal to provide the craft festival's executive committee with the financial information it requested. And Jeffrey spoke to me at length about the committee's concerns regarding the financial data that was supplied. I understand Jeffrey also made you aware that the committee feels the numbers were manipulated to support Dr. Kent's campaign to put an end to the festival."

Judith and Stewart both agreed that they were familiar with the committee's concerns.

"I need to confirm that Dr. Kent did, indeed, tell Donald not to supply information to Jeffrey and to determine whether or not Donald was involved with creating a misleading financial report. Since you have discussed these matters with Jeffrey, I would appreciate it if you would remain while I discuss them with Donald. Don't hesitate to ask questions if you think of something I have not covered."

Getting up from the table Adam went to the telephone, called Donald's office and asked him to return to the conference room. In a few minutes Donald joined them, puzzled as to why he had been called back and why the summons had come from the chairman of the board.

Adam explained that the Jordans had some questions about a donation made the previous September, and Donald remembered his telephone conversation with Stewart. Without waiting for anyone to make the request, he offered to print out a copy of Judith's file. He went to his office and returned with a two page document showing her donation history.

A quick perusal of the last notations confirmed the September donation and the October 19 designation change. No information had been added indicating the cooperative program had been reinstated as Roland had promised.

When asked by Adam if Judith should have been called about the change, Donald explained that an employee in Finance was unlikely to contact a donor when such a change was requested by Dr. Kent or even by Roland on behalf of the donor. "Our employees rarely deal with high level donors and would assume when such a request came from the museum director, it had the approval of the donor," he explained.

"May I ask a question?" Stewart looked at Adam.

"Of course," he replied.

"Something was said about the weathervane exhibition in reference to the designation change of my mother's donation. What do you know about that?"

Donald Lewis looked confused. "I don't recall that your donation was connected in any way to the weathervane exhibition," he said speaking to Judith. "I can check the list of donors, but it was a short list and I don't remember your name being on it."

After a moment's thought, he continued, "There was a donor who dropped out just as we were due to make the required deposit in mid-October, and Dr. Kent announced someone had anonymously stepped in to help. Was that you?" he asked. "Is that why the designation was changed?"

"It would seem," said Judith, "the answer to your question as to whether I anonymously helped with the deposit is 'yes.'"

From the tone of Judith's voice and the specificity of the questions, Donald realized something unethical had apparently occurred. And it must involve Dr. Kent - his initials were on the designation change, and he was not present in the conference room.

While malfeasance by the director was very serious for the museum, for Donald it meant no one in his department was being accused of wrong-doing. He was grateful for that.

Just as Donald was beginning to relax, Adam moved on to a different subject.

"I understand Jeffrey Longhurst, Chairman of the Craft Festival Executive Committee, requested certain financial figures after the committee's June meeting. Did anyone tell you not to provide them to him?"

Donald was not only startled by the sudden shift in subject but concerned about how his response might affect his employment at Summerston. However, he was an honorable man and would tell the truth no matter the consequences.

"After the June meeting, Dr. Kent told me if anyone on the committee asked for additional financial information, I was to contact him immediately because he would handle it," he admitted. "When Mr. Longhurst called and requested the complete line item budgets for the festival and the market, I called Dr. Kent as instructed."

"Was this unusual? Did Dr. Kent normally respond to requests for financial information from such committees?" asked Adam.

"No, I usually work directly with any board-appointed committee when financial information is required," responded Donald.

"I see," said Adam. "Now, the figures that were used for the hand-out distributed at that June meeting, who provided those?"

"My staff. I was asked by Roland to prepare comparisons of the festival and the market for the past five years using figures from the major headings in the budgets, such as personnel, publicity, facilities, catering - just the totals, no details for each category. And he wanted the same information for this spring's festival even though we did not have all of the figures," explained Donald.

"Did you see the actual financial report that was given to the committee?"

"Roland did not give me a copy of the hand-out, so I assumed it was what I gave to him. During the June meeting and the meeting this morning, I worked from my own copy of the staff report." As he responded to Adam, Donald began remembering the skepticism he had encountered when the figures were discussed. But Roland had warned him that the committee members might be very "touchy", as he put it, and had told Donald not to worry.

Adam looked at Stewart and Judith to see if they had any questions. When they shook their heads, he looked at Donald, "Thank you for your time. We do appreciate it. And you may wish to take a careful look at this," he added, handing Donald a sheet of paper from the table in front of him.

Realizing he was being dismissed, Donald said goodbye to everyone and left the room. Back in his office, he took a folder out of his desk file drawer. Removing the report his staff had prepared and placing it next to the hand-out Adam had just given him he discovered why he had been questioned about it. The budget figures his staff submitted and those supplied by Roland, bore little resemblance to one another.

FORTY-EIGHT

"**A**gain, my deepest apologies for what has happened. I do appreciate your not only bringing it to my attention but your helping me gather the necessary information for the board," Adam said to Judith and Stewart after Donald had left the conference room.

As Adam placed the file folder back into his brief case, Stewart responded, "We are grateful for your reacting to our concerns so quickly. I must confess, however, that I do wonder if we are the only ones whose donation has been misused."

"I share your concern."

"What happens now?" asked Judith.

"I will contact the museum trustees shortly and call an emergency meeting for this weekend. We can, of course, operate without a director for a few days. Truth be known, I suspect Elizabeth Markham, Dr. Kent's secretary, could run Summerston! She has been here long enough," he replied with a smile.

He shook hands with the Jordans and walked them down the stairs to the front door.

Marshalling his thoughts, Adam returned upstairs and went to Elizabeth's office where he thanked Henry

Davis and told him that he no longer needed him. As Henry went down the hall toward the stairs, Adam closed the door and seated himself in front of Elizabeth's desk.

Now in her late fifties, Elizabeth was an extremely capable assistant who worked well with the staff and trustees. She had been at the museum for thirty years, knew everything and everyone.

Even though it was a bit unorthodox, Adam had decided to talk with her about which staff members were least likely to have been confidents of Dr. Kent and Roland. He knew the last thing the museum needed was a repeat of the last two directors, even with someone who would temporarily hold the position. With her devotion to Summerston, he was sure she would not hesitate to assist him.

FORTY-NINE

About the same time a surprised Elizabeth Markham was meeting with Adam Payne, Brad Evans was rehearsing his lines for the latest campaign promoting Honey Nut Clusters cereal. *Nothing like playing second fiddle to a bunch of squirrels*, he mused with a wry smile. A classically trained actor with a long list of Broadway, Hollywood and television credits, he was now the spokesman for such companies as Pepsi and Southwest Airlines. Rather than his face, it was his voice that made him a very comfortable living.

At the age of sixty-two he enjoyed the work and found the anonymity less stressful. Tabloids and paparazzi took no interest in him which suited him just fine.

Looking down on the street from his spacious, second floor two bedroom apartment, Brad saw the mailman arrive.

After giving him time to sort everything, Brad descended the stairs and opened his mail box. Among the usual catalogs, inappropriate advertisements for aluminum gutters, and several personal notes from friends, he found a pale blue envelope with a familiar post office box number in the left hand corner.

Once back upstairs, he tore it open and found a

cashiers check for one thousand dollars. Attached was a small Post-it note on which was written "Well done, Trevor".

Not a bad paycheck for a few hours work, a delicious lunch at the elegant, five star Tasse d'Or and an interesting conversation with Adam Payne. *Thanks, Kate.*

And thank you, Jody. How fortunate that he had treated his niece and her roommate to dinner a month ago. An intern at Summerston, Jody had amused Brad with her imitation of Roland complaining about the misdirected seminar reservations. Little did she know how useful he would find her performance.

FIFTY

O n Monday, shortly after the museum opened, a shiny black crow perched on the windowsill looking in at Roland's now empty office. A gust of warm summer wind ruffled his feathers, and he lifted off into the sky. Gliding over the forest in full leaf and the green fields, he set down softly in the poplar tree next to the stonewall lining the driveway. From there he flew to the windowsill fronting a set of double windows, one of which was open to the gentle breeze.

Unaware of her observer, Adrienne perused last year's textile market timeline, making changes and adding entries. With little time between events, she had begun preparing for the market almost as soon as the craft festival ended. The soft bell tone alerted her to a new email. Glancing at her computer screen she noted an all-museum communication. Assuming it announced an upcoming staff lecture, new parking regulations or a sale in the gift shop, she somewhat absent-mindedly pulled it up on her screen. Still thinking about the timeline, she noticed the sender and heading out of the corner of her eye.

"Holy …!" she exclaimed. "Elinor," she yelled, startling the crow who had been contemplating a hop into the room to grab one of the pretzels in an open bag near the window.

But she needn't have yelled. Elinor was already standing in her office doorway having rushed up the stairs after she read the email, herself.

"What do you think is going on?" she asked, somewhat out of breath.

"I know what I hope it means," replied Adrienne. "I wonder who might have some information."

"Someone at PR must know the details if something major is happening, but I don't think you want to try anyone there. What about Carl in Finance? I don't know how, but he seems to know things before anyone else does," suggested Elinor.

Answering on the second ring, Carl did, indeed, have some information.

"Lou, the security guard who was on patrol Friday told me that Henry Davis asked to be notified when Roland and Dr. Kent left Summerston. And all of the guards were given instructions to let Henry know immediately if their cars were seen on the grounds again."

FIFTY-ONE

While Carl imparted what he knew to Adrienne and Elinor, Thurston Wilde was on the telephone from his hotel room in Pittsburgh. Upon returning from breakfast on Saturday morning, he had found a frantic message from Roland on his phone's voicemail. Almost incomprehensible, Roland had fumed about being framed and deceived and needing Thurston to contact some of his important friends to help him out. Busy with preparations for his speech to the historical society's annual dinner on Sunday, he had not acted on Roland's call until this morning.

"Joseph, Thurston here. That position with the Harrington Museum you described to me last week when you called. I'll take you up on your offer. I can fly out today and meet with your board this week. In the meantime, I'll email my resumé."

An hour later, sitting in Elizabeth Markham's office, Adam Payne was putting the finishing touches to a news release. This announcement, more lengthy than the one he had emailed to the staff earlier, would be sent not only to museum employees but to local and national media. Wary of the public relations division, he had decided to prepare the statement himself and have Elizabeth send it.

Across the courtyard, meeting with his Research Department staff in a conference room on the third floor of the museum building, Jeremy Aycres was not doodling. He was, to be blunt, in a state of shock. Had he drawn a bird it would have been lying on its back with glazed eyes and its feet in the air. As he finished speaking, the room broke into applause and cheers.

His assistant reached into a bag at his feet, stood, and ceremonially presented Jeremy with the small sparrow-like bird that usually sat in Jeremy's office. Only now it wore a tiny gold paper crown, slightly askew.

7850168R0

Made in the USA
Lexington, KY
17 December 2010